Hard Candy 2:

Secrets Uncovered

🔹Prairie State College

Back to Books

Purchased with Library Services and Technology Act funds provided by the Illinois State Library.

FY 2013

Hard Candy 2:
Secrets Uncovered

Amaleka McCall

www.urbanbooks.net

Urban Books, LLC
78 East Industry Court
Deer Park, NY 11729

ISBN 13: 978-1-60162-496-3
ISBN 10: 1-60162-496-4

First Printing February 2012
Printed in the United States of America

10 9 8 7 6 5 4 3 2 1

Distributed by Kensington Publishing Corp.
Submit Wholesale Orders to:
Kensington Publishing Corp.
C/O Penguin Group (USA) Inc.
Attention: Order Processing
405 Murray Hill Parkway
East Rutherford, NJ 07073-2316
Phone: 1-800-526-0275
Fax: 1-800-227-9604

To know your enemy,
you must become your enemy.

—Sun Tzu, *The Art of War*

Previously in *Hard Candy:*

Candice, Junior and Tuck speechlessly watched the scene unfold. Uncle Rock turned around and began walking back toward them. Tuck gripped his gun tightly; he couldn't be sure that Barton hadn't been hired to take him out also. Uncle Rock walked right past Tucker, coughing fiercely as blood dribbled from his lips.

"Uncle Rock!" Candice cried out, moving toward him.

"Stay there!" Uncle Rock screamed, halting her steps.

"Yo, this is some straight-outta-movie shit. All I wanna do is take my fuckin' dough and get the fuck outta here. I can't have my moms burying two sons!" Junior exclaimed.

"Wait!" Uncle Rock yelled at him.

Then he said, "Candy, what you read in my last will and testament was true. I am dying. I have cancer. I did love someone at one time, and that love bore a son. His name is Joseph Carson, but his mother called him Junior." Uncle Rock leaned over to cough up more blood.

"What, nigga?" Junior barked, lifting his gun. A spark of anger ignited inside him. Staring at Rock, Junior remembered him as the old dude hanging with Easy, when Easy gave Junior a job.

"You fuckin' punk-ass bitch nigga! You let me go years without a father? Suffering at the hands of Broady's fucked-up pops . . . watching my moms get her ass beat up. You watched me go fuckin' hungry and have to steal from the store, and you ain't do shit." Junior choked on his words. He was a man, and he wasn't going to let no tears fall, especially at no soap opera shit like this.

Uncle Rock spit up more blood.

"I should kill your fuckin' ass right here!" Junior growled.

Candice raised her gun. "I don't think so. . . . He saved your fuckin' life today," Candice grumbled.

"Candy . . . let him do it. Let him do it before they come for me," Uncle Rock rasped out.

"What are you talkin' about?" Candice asked.

"I'm dying, anyway. . . . Shoot me now. Don't let them have the satisfaction," Uncle Rock begged.

"No!" Candice screamed.

"All of you have to go. Get out of here. . . . Run. It's never over when you have information about the government," Uncle Rock wheezed.

"You can go with me. I have the money . . . from— from . . . Daddy," Candice pleaded. She couldn't stand losing her uncle. Not now.

"Candy, you especially need to go. They will have a bounty on your head. You need to run," Uncle Rock said.

Before any of them could blink, Uncle Rock looked at Candy and let his gun hand drop to his leg. He fired a single shot. She opened her mouth to scream, but it happened too fast.

"Noooo!" Candice hollered.

Uncle Rock's body dropped to the ground, but his eyes were still open. Blood leaked from his mouth, *but he was still trying to talk. Candice ran to him. She knew she only had ten seconds or less. Uncle Rock had taught her about this very moment. Candice bent down at his side, but she could see the blood soaking through his pant leg.*

"Why?" Candice screamed, trying to apply pressure on Uncle Rock's wound.

"Because . . . I—I . . . love you," Uncle Rock managed. Then his head lulled to the side. His eyes were open and vacant.

"What the fuck!" Tuck huffed, bending down next to Candice. She looked at him pitifully. Tears ran down her face in buckets.

"He shot himself in the femoral artery," Candice cried. Tuck grabbed her around the shoulders.

"There's nothing you can do for him, Candy. He did it all for you," Tuck comforted. Junior walked over and stood over the man who had just confessed to being his father. He wasn't going to shed a tear.

"Yo, Tuck . . . who the fuck are you?" Junior asked.

Tuck stood up, face-to-face with Junior.

"I am Avon Tucker, a DEA agent who got set up by his own partner," Tuck confessed.

Candice looked at him strangely. She was too overwhelmed with a mixture of emotions to be mad. They had both operated under false pretenses.

"So you were tryin'a take me down?" Junior asked.

"That was my assignment, but it was all a fuckin' joke. You've been working for the government, anyway," Tuck told him.

A loud chopping sound could be heard overhead. The helicopters were hovering just above them.

"They're coming. Barton warned us. We need to get out of here," Tuck said urgently.

"What about Uncle Rock's body?" Candice asked sadly.

"They will make this one big crime scene. Once they do their investigation, they will contact his next of kin," Tuck told her.

"Which is you," Candice commented to Junior. The sound of the helicopters was getting closer, and sirens could be heard in the distance. They all started to disperse like rats in an alley. Candice went left, Junior went straight ahead, and Tuck remained back. Tuck was the only one who didn't have a ride. He watched Candice walk toward her car and disappear from the darkened street. Junior quickly got into his truck and peeled off.

Within five minutes Tuck was surrounded. He lifted his hands in the air in surrender.

"I am Avon Tucker, DEA agent," he screamed out. One of the black Impala doors swung open.

"Are you still a DEA agent, Avon Tucker?" Dana Carlisle called out.

Chapter 1

The Aftermath

Candice pressed her foot lead heavy on the gas pedal and drove away from the crime scene like her life depended on it. Pulling up near her apartment building, Candice wiped the tears off her cheek. She had to focus on getting the hell out of the area, like Uncle Rock had instructed. *You're a big girl. . . . It's time to grow up. It's just you against them. C'mon, Candy, you can do this. Make Uncle Rock proud.* Candice gave herself a stern pep talk as she exhaled and put the gear into park. She rushed out of the car, whirling her head around in every direction, making sure she wasn't being watched. With her heart racing, Candice took the steps leading to her apartment two at a time. This was one of those times she had to heed Uncle Rock's lessons about being stealthy, accurate, focused and fast when on a mission.

Candice reached the floor where her apartment was located in the old high-rise building. The hallway was empty. Candice's hands were shaking badly; she could barely get the key into the lock. Finally the lock clicked and she pushed her way inside the familiar doorway. Before she could get her bearings, her jaw went slack with shock.

"These bastards!" Candice growled as she moved slowly. She took in the nightmarish scene and instinctively fumbled in her bag until she located her two favorite weapons, a .40-caliber Glock 22 and a .357 SIG Sauer. Her fingers instinctively chose the Glock.

Shaking her head from left to right, trying to make sense of what she was seeing, Candice slowly moved through the now-unfamiliar space filled with the debris of her ruined personal effects. Candice kicked a path clear and roved the rooms with her protection gripped tightly. Everything in her apartment had been turned upside down. The living-room furniture was no more. The end tables and coffee table lay splintered in pieces; her sofa lay on its back and had been sliced like a pig in a slaughterhouse. The kitchen had been trashed as well. The cabinets hung open, their contents swiped from the shelves onto the floor and counters. Even the drawers had been pulled from their slots, with their contents dumped out unceremoniously onto the laminate floor.

A creaking sound caused Candice to jump. Her nostrils flared as she eyed the hallway leading to her bedroom and placed a two-handed, thumb-over-thumb grip on her weapon. Someone must still be here. The way she held her weapon now, and moved her body, made her think of Uncle Rock. *Fuck!* she screamed inside her head. Her vision began to blur as the tears burned behind her eyes. Biting down into her jaw, Candice moved slowly toward the back of her apartment, where her bedroom was located. In there was a safe, which contained her life savings. Candice swallowed hard and forced her legs forward. Her survival instincts began to take over. She had to get that money, and get the hell out of there fast.

Moving with her back up against the walls, in case someone was still lurking about, Candice finally made it to the bedroom doorway. With her gun leading the way, she dipped her head inside quickly and backed out, just as fast. She said a quick, silent prayer and rushed through the entranceway. As she entered the room, glass crunched under her feet. Candice stopped breathing for a minute. She bent down and picked up the shattered photo frame, which contained a portrait of her slain family. Her heart jerked in her chest as she looked at the jagged lines from the broken glass running across her father's face. How ironic that his face was sliced in half by the glass, much like the double life he had led as a drug-dealing government mule. Quickly coming back to the reality of her situation, Candice whirled around in the middle of the floor, with her weapon pointed out in front of her. It appeared that whoever had been in her apartment was long gone.

Breathing a sigh of relief, Candy tried to unravel the mystery behind her trashed apartment.

What the fuck were they looking for? Candice wondered as she trod carefully around her once-immaculately-clean bedroom. The box spring lay exposed and her mattress was on the floor, sliced and diced, with the cotton spilling out as if someone had been digging in the middle of it. Her closet had been emptied of its contents, with her clothes, shoes and handbags tossed into a pile on the floor. Her desk had been turned over, and her laptop screen smashed. The cork message board that was usually above her desk, which had contained pictures of Junior and his crew, was also broken into three pieces. All of the pictures had been removed. Who would want to steal those pictures?

Maybe Uncle Rock was right. Maybe the government was after her because of the skills she possessed and the information she was privy to as a result of her association with Rock. Or maybe Junior was coming after her to avenge the death of his brother, Broady. The conspiracy theories abounded in Candice's mind, but she didn't have time to give them any real thought. Her first priority was locating the safe in the bottom of her closet. Frantically she tossed aside the pile of clothes and shoes that covered the closet floor. She blew out a cleansing breath; then she noticed that, strangely enough, the medium-sized gray fireproof safe was still there, seemingly untouched. Candice was no dummy. The safe wasn't still there because the intruders wanted her to have money to live. The whole thing reeked of a setup; whoever had wrecked her apartment wanted to make a statement, but they also wanted her to get away.

Candice entered the safe combination, but her hands were unsteady and she had to spin the wheel a couple of times before it opened. Once the lock clicked, Candice pulled the small metal door back. She let out a long sigh of relief when she noticed that the money her father had left her—what she hadn't spent keeping up with Junior and his hustling crew—was still there. All of the ammunition was still there as well. Money, guns and bullets—that was all she had left in the world. It was also all she had conditioned herself to believe she needed. The safe would be too cumbersome and heavy to try to carry out of the apartment, so she quickly emptied the contents into a duffel bag.

Fuck love. Fuck having a family. Candice told herself she was about to step out into the world alone. Before she left, Candice carefully placed the picture of her family on top of the stacks of money in the bag, picked up her loaded weapon, and raced for the front door. With a quick, last look around, Candice knew she would never again set eyes on this place. She was about to embark on a whole new life, and she was painfully aware that she was no longer the hunter, but the hunted.

***

After almost being killed by Candy and watching Rock take his life, Junior fled the scene and headed straight to his mother's house. He had rushed up the front steps of his mother's house, unable to get a handle on his feelings. How could his mother have so willfully deceived him about who the fuck his father was? He entered the brownstone furious like a gust of wind around a tornado.

"Ma!" Junior called out as he stalked through the hallway leading to his mother's kitchen. "Ma! Where you at?" Junior belted out, his voice a quaking baritone. No response. He finally found his mother sitting at the kitchen table, with her head down, clutching a wadded-up napkin.

"Ma, didn't you hear me calling you?" Junior huffed, his tone going higher with irritation. "We gotta talk! I need to ask you some questions right now, and I want the truth!" he boomed, slamming his fist on the table. He was ready to lay into his mother about who his father was, but his plan was quickly derailed.

Slowly raising her head, Betty Carson looked up at her eldest son. Fear was evident on her face. Junior halted in his tracks at the sight of his mother; he rushed to her side.

"Ma, what happened to you?" he barked incredulously. His mother sobbed even harder and quickly lowered her head. "Ma . . ." Junior's tone had softened; sympathy was tracing his words.

His legs felt weak and something deep in the center of his chest ached. He placed his hand under his mother's chin and lifted her face so he could get a better look. Junior let out an animalistic moan as he examined every inch of her paper bag–colored skin. Her left eye was swollen shut with dark purple and deep red rings forming around the outside of it. Her nose was red and swollen, with crusted blood rimming the inside of her nostrils; dark welts were rising on her cheeks.

"What happened to you?" Junior asked again, his heart thumping wildly at the idea of someone harming his mother.

"What did you do? What did you do to your brother? What did you do to me?" His mother suddenly came alive, her voice a high-pitched screech. The bitterness in her tone caused Junior to take a few steps backward.

"What are you talking about?" Junior replied, pleading ignorance.

"They told me what you did! They came here and did this to me! They told me, you were the one who killed Broady, and now they are gonna kill you and me!" Betty belted out, unable to control her wails now.

Junior swallowed and bit down so hard into his cheek that he drew his own blood. The acrid taste seemingly fueled his homicidal feelings. He felt like wrecking shit around him. The heat of his anger rose from his toes and climbed up into his soul.

"Who was it?" he managed to croak out as his chest rose and fell rapidly. He balled his fists in an attempt to keep his rage at bay.

"He said his name was Phil and that you killed his baby brother, so he killed yours. Said you tortured that boy, a twelve-year-old boy, and then killed him!" Betty sobbed, accusing her son through her one good eye. "Oh, Junior . . . I saw that story on the news!" she wailed some more. "Are you out there killing people, Junior?" she asked in a low whisper, her eyes pleading for an explanation.

Junior stood mutely at her side.

"Oh, God!" his mother called on the Heavenly Father for understanding and comfort.

Junior suddenly felt too weak to stand. He flopped down onto one of the kitchen chairs. His mother took his disregard for her question as an admission of guilt, but there was no way that he would tell his mother that Broady was actually to blame for most of what had happened. Junior's body felt hot, and his healing gunshot wound began to throb from the adrenaline pulsing through his body. His head pounded with a migraine-caliber headache at the base of his skull. He squeezed his eyes shut and let the silence in the room settle around him—the calm before the storm.

Phil, the leader of the uptown crew of drug dealers, had crossed the line when he touched Junior's mother. Junior and Phil had called a truce years ago. It was agreed that Junior would run the Brooklyn street empire, and Phil would remain Uptown. They were supposed to be peers in the game, on the same level, but Phil had reached down too far. Junior would never have thought to touch any member of Phil's family. Junior had even told Phil that it was Junior's hotheaded brother, Broady, who had harmed Phil's little brother, Carmelo. Junior thought Phil understood, but now he knew different.

Junior's eyes were ablaze, and his nostrils were flared. He felt the strong desire to grab his mother into his arms and comfort her with a hug. He hadn't hugged his mother since he was a small child. Betty was never real big on affection. It was a wall that her children simply acknowledged as insurmountable. Though she never told them with words or actions that she loved them, they knew she did in her own way. But perhaps this urge to comfort his mother was merely an excuse to receive it in return. Obviously, sorting out the truth with his mother about his real father was a conversation Junior would have to have another day and time.

He couldn't wait to get back to the streets. He had tried his best to prevent a war from happening, but Phil and his crew had pushed Junior to his limit.

"I've told you all that I know!" Avon Tucker screamed, clenching his fists so tight his knuckles paled. He looked around at all of the accusatory faces and bit down into his jaw. This was some bullshit. It had been two weeks since the shootings that had claimed his partner's life, and he was still being interrogated as if he were the bad guy.

The DEA, NYPD and, of course, the FBI had converged on the scene, each wanna-be-in-charge acronym vying for jurisdiction over the scene. Avon had raised his hands like a suspect, his street clothes, obligatory diamond Jesus piece and long chain not helping him make the case that he was actually an undercover Drug Enforcement Administration agent.

Immediately following the shooting, Avon was treated like a victim. At first, he was given time to "think things over." He was taken under the wing of the Employee Assistance Program. This was called the "get your story together" time among law enforcement officers—a week's worth of meetings with EAP shrinks, and strict isolation from the media and the U.S. Attorney's Office investigators. In fact, this was his first "on the record" interview regarding the incident, and everyone wanted a piece of it.

Avon's role as "victim" somehow blurred into "suspect" as probing, accusatory questions seemed to become the order of the day. Where was Tucker when Brubaker had been shot? Had he identified himself as a DEA agent? How long had he been undercover? Wasn't it true he had committed violations of the undercover rule, and only Brubaker had knowledge of this? Did he blame Brubaker for the first shooting incident of his career?

That question had struck a raw nerve with Avon. He didn't like anyone mentioning the accident he'd been involved in that resulted in a fifteen-year-old unarmed boy dying during an early-morning drug raid, early in his career. It was a memory he couldn't shake anytime someone brought it up. It had been a highly dangerous and high-profile drug raid on the home of a well-known drug dealer that had changed things for Avon.

Unfortunately, the DEA's confidential informant had provided the wrong address. When Avon's unit rammed the door of the home and entered tactically, there was a lot of screaming and running. As they worked to clear the house, Avon and Brad Brubaker searched the back rooms to make sure everyone was accounted for. In one of the bedrooms, Avon could hear someone breathing hard in the closet. Brubaker put his fingers to his lips to indicate silence, and the two approached the closet on deft feet. Brubaker pulled back the closet door for Avon to clear, and a young boy jumped out with a black crowbar raised in his hand. Avon, in knee-jerk reaction, overreacted and let off a single shot. The boy died later that day at the hospital. There was a huge public fallout. Everyone in the city wanted Avon's head on a platter; firing him wasn't going to be enough. Avon was ultimately vindicated of any wrongdoing because he was able to articulate his perceived threat—the boy could've just as easily had a gun. But Avon's name was forever tarnished by the incident.

All of the people in the room now were supposed to be on his side; but the earlier shoot-the-shit atmosphere had been replaced by a harsher, more attack dog format. Now Avon sat in the hot seat and was forced to defend his honor and his actions. Had Avon set Brubaker up to die, after finding Brubaker having an affair with his wife? Did he know Joseph Barton personally? Did he want Brubaker dead because he would expose Avon for committing crimes while undercover? And finally, why didn't he try to save Brubaker?

Apparently "no" or "I don't know" were not satisfactory responses to the investigators. Instead, they would simply rephrase their questions to try to trip up Avon. It was a law enforcement philosophy—the more times someone had to tell the story, the more holes they might find. And, of course, these were holes that might be filled with lies.

Letting out a long sigh, Avon roughly rubbed his hands over his face in exasperation. It was going to be a very long day.

"Like I said, Joseph 'Rock' Barton was the shooter. He was the older guy on the scene. He said that he was working for some fuckin' body inside of this agency—the DEA!" Avon's voice rose an octave or two, startling his fresh-out-of-law-school Federal Law Enforcement Officer's Association–funded attorney.

Avon couldn't help it; his emotions were on a hair trigger. He had been shot at, betrayed and hunted while working undercover on a case that was never intended to go anywhere. And now he was suddenly a suspect in some fictional conspiracy.

Avon closed his eyes and placed his palms flat on the table. In an unnervingly calm voice, he continued, "Again, Barton walked over to Brad Brubaker. He pulled his weapon out and said these exact words, 'You can't be that stupid. . . . Your backup is not coming. They hired me for one last cleaner job . . . but it wasn't for who you thought. Did you think the government would laud you for being a traitor? Did you think they would promote you, trust you and respect you after you threw your own partner to the wolves—betraying him, lying on him, committing murders and putting them on your partner? Did you really think they would kill another federal agent to get him out of your way? Couldn't you see that while you thought Tucker's case was all one big red herring, you were being duped?' Then he shot Brubaker in his head." Avon looked up at the ceiling, as if recalling the entire scene from some distant place in his mind. He wanted to finish his recount of the events with his own personal opinion that the traitorous rat bastard deserved to have his head blown off, but he refrained himself from doing so, knowing those types of statements would make him look like he wanted his partner dead.

"Do you wanna take a break? Um . . . I think my client needs a break," Avon's pimply-faced Georgetown-graduate lawyer stammered, sounding just like one of those clichéd television series attorneys. No one in the room paid him any mind. "Okay . . . may-maybe not." The attorney shrank back down onto his seat.

The DEA interrogators who surrounded Avon turned quiet; it was a tactic Avon recognized. Silence usually unnerved guilty suspects, making them feel the need to fill up the silence with words, which would inevitably cause a slipup. Avon was silent too. He was trying to read them. Were they appeased? Were they still suspicious? The tension in the room was stifling. Some of the interrogators' faces had looked as if Avon had just announced that he had a terminal illness, while others looked less surprised and more suspicious.

A tall, square-shouldered white man broke from the group and walked over and placed one leg on the edge of the table, where Avon sat. The man leaned in so close—

Avon could smell stale coffee on the man's breath. "And you didn't attempt to save your fellow agent's life?" the man asked again, his bulldog jaw shaking with emphasis as he spat the words in Avon's face.

Avon slammed his hand on the small, wobbly silver table, causing the man to quickly remove his leg and stand erect. Avon jutted his pointer finger toward the beefy man. He was tired of the accusatory tone of this whole circus.

"Are you listening to what I am saying? Brubaker tried to have me killed. He left me undercover with some of the most dangerous drug dealers in New York, and then he went and fucked my wife—just for the hell of it! Somebody paid Barton to kill him, and then Barton turned the gun on himself! But it wasn't me! This entire fuckin' movie-like conspiracy is much bigger than me. I shouldn't be the one explaining it all. Somebody should be explaining to me why I was thrown in the thick of a fuckin' government cluster fuck, and why my case agent was a crooked motherfucker who was probably working for you! Not only could I have been killed, but a lot of innocent people died because of this little fucked-up game you're running here!" Avon barked back, the muscles cording in the chocolate skin of his neck. They had finally penetrated his resolve.

The interrogators eased back and softened their tones. Another tactic. Now they'd play nice guy and try to get some type of admission, if not a confession. They'd never seen any guilty person speak with so much conviction.

"Agent Tucker, we know this is hard. We just need the facts. Tell us one more time where you stood. What about the girl?" the lone female of the bunch chimed in, her eyes soft and placating.

Avon's face softened when he pictured Candy's face in his mind's eye. He had been thinking about her non-stop. He wondered where she had gone and if she was in any danger. Avon rested his elbows on the table and placed his bald head in his hands. He had to admit, as young as Candy was, she had done something to his heart. He had tried to tell himself that the night they shared together was purely a result of finding out his wife and partner were playing house during his absence, but Avon admitted to himself that he really had feelings for Candy. After the night they'd shared, he could not stop thinking about her. He felt sick, crazy even. Candy was a young girl, and he was a married man; yet she was a recurring thought.

Everyone in the room seemed to be suspended in time waiting for Tucker to answer the question. Avon opened his mouth to tell them the story again. He would pick and choose what he told them about Candy.

A loud knock, echoing through the door, interrupted his thoughts. Avon's shoulders went from tense to relaxed; the knocking was a welcome distraction from the line of questioning. Everyone else turned toward the thick metal door as well, unsure of what course of action to take. The female interrogator stood up in a law enforcement stance—her legs were shoulder width apart; her hands up and at the ready, like she needed to be prepared for Armageddon.

One of the DEA interrogators stalked over to the door and snatched it back like he was ready to chew out whoever was interrupting their show. The man standing behind the door walked into the room—it was like Moses parting the Red Sea to reach the Promised Land. Time seemed to stand still.

"There will be no more questions, unless we are the ones asking them," Grayson Stokes announced firmly, his voice raspy like his throat was covered with phlegm. Avon's lawyer shot up from his seat; all of his papers flopped all over the floor, as he forgot they were on his lap. "Wait a minute, my client—" he interjected. "Shut it!" Stokes snapped, pointing a curved finger at the attorney. The attorney snapped his mouth shut; it was as if the man had put him under some sort of spell. All of the agents in the room reacted as if they were a group of teens who had just gotten busted at an underage drinking party.

"If you ever want to earn a paycheck from the United States government again, I suggest you get the fuck out of here," the old man hissed, pointing a yellow fingernail. Immediately taking the man for an authority figure, the rank-and-file agents all began to scatter.

"Everybody leave," the man demanded, gazing at the attorney and the few brave investigators lingering in the room. They silently cleared out, though many of the faces looked none too pleased.

"Wait a minute here. He works for the DEA and we have the—" one of the bolder DEA agents dared to challenge. However, the icy stare and stone-faced grill he received from Stokes had him taking three steps backward toward the door.

Stokes's *Men in Black*–looking escorts waited for the attorney to gather his papers before ushering him out of the room. Talk about walking clichés.

"Are you going to be all right?" Avon's lawyer turned and asked from the doorway.

"Didn't I say get the fuck out of here!" the old man barked. His chest suddenly erupted and he exploded into a fit of coughing. His escorts each grabbed one of the attorney's arms and shoved him through the door.

Avon started to stand up too, but the man clapped one of his liver-spotted hands on Avon's shoulder.

"Not you, Agent Tucker . . . or should I just call you Avon?" the old man asked, forcing Avon back down onto the chair. The metal door slammed shut with a ring of finality.

"Look, I don't know where you're from, or what you want, but I know I have the right to an attorney," Avon demanded, starting to stand up again.

The dark shade–wearing escorts moved in closer.

Avon slumped back on the chair. "I am not under arrest . . . or am I? If I am, I need to hear my Miranda warnings, now," Avon snapped.

Stokes let out a sarcastic snort. With his hazy, silvery, medicine-dilated pupils trained on Avon's face, the man sized him up.

"You're right. You're not under arrest and you do have certain rights, under certain laws. But at what cost would you exercise your right to leave?" he grumbled, reaching into the left side of his suit.

Instinctively, Avon went to his waist. He found nothing there, of course. The old man chuckled, and then another fit of coughing.

"Did you think I was reaching for a gun, Agent Tucker?" the man asked. "I have something far more valuable to you," he corrected, flicking two glossy 8x10 photographs on the table in front of Avon.

The photographs floated onto the table and slid perfectly into place in front of Avon; it was like a special magic trick. Avon sucked in his breath. He felt like someone had kicked him in the chest. He stared down, unable to peel his eyes away from them. He was experiencing changes in his body chemistry that he couldn't explain—sweat seemed to pop up on his forehead, like unwanted dandelions on a fresh green lawn, and his breathing felt labored. His ears began ringing and he lifted his hand to his chest. He felt like someone had sucked all of the air out of the room. Avon snapped his head up from the pictures. It was as if someone had pulled it up abruptly with an invisible string. His eyes hooded over and he set his jaw squarely.

"Who the fuck are you? And what the fuck do you want?"

Avon gritted his teeth, eyeing Stokes evilly. The man remained silent as he placed another picture down on the table. It was a picture of Avon and Candy leaving Kings County Hospital together on the night her friend Shana had died. Avon's heart jerked in his chest, and he couldn't stop staring at all of the pictures now. Obviously, this old bastard had been watching him very closely.

"I didn't think you'd be interested in leaving after you saw those. Listen, Special Agent Avon Tucker . . . Tuck, the drug dealer, or Tucker—or whatever the fuck you want to be called these days," the man said snidely. Moving close to Avon's ear, he leaned over Avon's shoulder so that Avon could smell his Ralph Lauren Safari cologne, cigar smoke on his clothes and his breath. "This should be easy. I am Grayson Stokes. I used to work with Joseph 'Rock' Barton. Sound familiar? I thought it would. Barton trained your little friend Candice Hardaway . . . or maybe you call her 'Candy.' See, Agent Tucker, we have a few friends in common and I need you to do something for me. It has to be you, or it wouldn't even be worth it," he said, moving away to see Avon's expression and reaction.

Avon's face was drawn into a scowl and his jaws rocked feverishly as he ground his molars together. He didn't like this old bastard mentioning Candy.

"You don't have to like it. I know you already know some things about Operation Easy In and Joseph Barton, but not nearly enough to think you know the entire story. You do what I say, and you get to see these little angel faces again," the man proposed.

"What do you want? I don't know shit," Avon said through gritted teeth, his nostrils flaring.

"The girl . . . Candy . . . I want her, and you're going to be the one to bring her to me," the old man said sternly, using his head to signal one of his men to surround Avon. "Are you in? Do we have a deal, Agent Tucker?" Grayson Stokes asked, reshuffling the pictures in front of him.

Avon Tucker was a captive audience now; and he knew no matter what his answer was, he would be making a deal with the devil.

Chapter 2

Going Ghost

Three Weeks Later

Tears drain from the corners of Candy's eyes and she is shivering all over. For some reason she is strangely aware of the cold, wet grass under her knees as she puts pressure on them in front of the tombstone. The feeling reminds her of the cold, empty feeling she had in her heart since the death of Uncle Rock. She can't believe he is dead. She also can't believe that she has returned to Brooklyn after she has been warned not to come back.

Candice doesn't care about the potential danger of her return. She has never had a chance to pay her respects to her family, but she feels an overwhelming need to come see the resting place of her uncle.

At the age of fourteen, Candice had lost her family, and she misses all of them deeply. However, she'd had her uncle Rock to comfort her after she found her entire family massacred.

Now she kneels at Uncle Rock's grave, painfully aware that she is alone. She is left to fend for herself. Candice pulls off the little white plastic top from the steaming hot cup of green tea and pours it slowly on the green and brown grass in front of Uncle Rock's tombstone. "I know you must miss your daily cup of green tea," Candice whispers, her voice shaky.

Candice feels a rush of wind on the back of her neck, which causes the tiny hairs there to stand up. She is sure it was Uncle Rock giving her a hug. She isn't really religious, but she starts to say a silent prayer.

Just then she hears the faint sound of leaves crunching behind her. Alert, she places her hand into her bag and grips her Glock 22. Her heart begins to pound against her chest bone as the sound seems to get closer. Candice grips her gun more tightly.

It is them, she is sure.

Slowly she begins to stand up. She lets her bag stay on the ground and she lifts up her weapon out of it. With her chest heaving up and down, Candice is fully aware of the person's presence at her back. She attempts to turn around, but it is too late. More than one person rushes her at the same time.

She can hear a man's muffled voice: "We told you we would find you if you ever returned."

"Agh!" She lets out a short-lived scream.

Then blackness.

"Oh shit!" Candice jumped out of her sleep and out of the bed. She whirled around on the balls of her feet, trying to get her bearings. Her body was covered in sweat and her ears were ringing. Clutching her chest, Candice flopped down on the side of the bed. She exhaled and looked at her gun on the hotel's nightstand. The dreams were worse now than ever before. She didn't even realize she had dozed off in the middle of the day. It had been a long, exhausting day spent buying wigs and costumes, and perfecting her disguise. Candice shook off the nightmare and walked into the hotel's bathroom.

"Can't believe I have to sleep in this stuff too," she whispered to herself. She stared at her image in the large vanity mirror hanging over the hotel bathroom's sink. She hardly recognized herself anymore. The wet and wavy lace front wig she wore was cut into a short, high-low bob; it was also at least five shades lighter than her normal dark brown hair. She adjusted the wig a few times and secured it by applying the lace front glue, like the little Asian lady in the store had told her to do. Candice shook her head left to right to make sure her wig wouldn't go flying off at random. Candice was so accustomed to having long hair; the change seemed drastic. But that was exactly the look she was going for. She leaned in close to the mirror to examine her new eye color—gray. These new cat eyes were courtesy of a brand-new pair of light-reflecting colored contacts that accented her natural color with just rims of gray. Candice turned to the side to examine the most drastic change in her identity shift. She touched her midsection, lifting her new overhang gut. Candice had to laugh at the sixty extra pounds around her stomach and sides, thanks to the fat suit she'd purchased from a costume store. She looked like an overweight Spanish woman as she pulled up the thigh pads that made her usually long, slender legs look grossly misshapen and riddled with cellulite.

Walking back out into the hotel room, Candice couldn't help but take another look at the collage she had created on the far left wall. With her hands on her hips, she stood in front of what she considered her new target board. She had taped a bunch of photographs, names and maps together in perfect pattern—a masterpiece in her mind.

Moving her eyes across each face, she studied each name and each place, making sure she would not forget the real individuals responsible for the massacre of her family.

"Rolando DeSosa . . . sons Arellio and Guillermo," Candice read aloud, for probably the one hundredth time. "You, Guillermo, are not that bad-looking, still not my type," she said with a tsk. "I guess it really doesn't matter, though, now . . . does it?" she continued as if the man in the photo could somehow hear her. She rolled her new eyes and smiled. "We will meet soon; and when we do, your ass is mine," she murmured.

It had been easier than she'd thought to find information on the Internet about DeSosa and his family. Candice had to doubt what her Uncle Rock had told her before his suicide about DeSosa working for the CIA. In her assessment there was just way too much information out there about the supposedly notorious man. Candice had found information on several of DeSosa's past arrests, his current and past real estate listings, his legitimate business holdings, court documents from past indictments containing his whereabouts, his children's names and even some of the names of his many mistresses. The fact that this information was so readily available made her skeptical about Rock's claims—after all, the government was quite capable of planting information if it suited their needs.

Candice clicked on her laptop and inserted her Rosetta Stone CD. She needed to get her accent down pat. Uncle Rock had taught her basic Spanish while he had homeschooled her, but she wanted to be great before she set out on her new mission. Once she infiltrated DeSosa's circle, she needed to be able to keep up with every conversation within her earshot.

Picking up her laptop, Candice walked over to the bed and settled her back against the headboard, with the laptop on her thighs. As she focused on the computer screen, the photograph of her family on the nightstand fell silently to the floor. The air in the room seemed to become lead heavy. Keeping her emotions in check was no easy feat. Now that Rock was gone, the only link to her past was this solitary 3x5 family photo.

Candice flopped down on the side of the bed and picked up the portrait. On the one hand, she wanted to turn it on its face so that all of the smiling faces would stop taunting her; but on the other hand, she needed to see them like she had for the past four and a half years. She looked at each face and the anger she had previously felt in the years since their deaths finally eased into real sorrow—pure mourning. The photo had been her talisman for many years, keeping the kindling lit under her seething anger and need for revenge.

Candice would often look to the picture, promising her family members that she would get revenge—no matter what it cost her. In her mind she had played, over and over, the gruesome murder scene that she'd stumbled upon at fourteen: Her mother's open, vacant eyes, dead and unforgiving, as they gazed back at her. Her baby sister's naked, badly beaten body sprawled before her. Both of her brothers laying on the floor— one with a slit throat, and the other with his head almost decapitated. But the most crushing image was that of her father, who was facedown, with the entire back of his head blown off.

Candice didn't even realize she was gnawing on her bottom lip as her eyes carefully gazed upon each face. The picture had an entirely new look now. Everyone looked different in her eyes. Gone was the innocence of a family of victims. Now, with the information shared with Candy by Uncle Rock prior to his death, she saw them with fresh eyes. Each one, with the exception of her baby sister, harbored secrets that were now being uncovered.

"Your father made a deal with the government, and there was no turning back. Rolando DeSosa, the man who supplied your father with all of the drugs, worked for the CIA, and so did I." Those had been Uncle Rock's final words before he took his own life.

Candice's temples throbbed as she searched the recesses of her mind, digging into her memory for some clue, some inkling, that would help her understand her father's double life. Why had her father treaded such dangerous territory, putting his own family into the fray? Tears fell on the shattered glass that covered the picture. Candice used her trembling thumb to swipe the glass clean. Her sweet baby sister stared back at her with a toothy grin. Candice's chest felt tight. She leaned her head back and closed her eyes, racking her brain for memories that would bring her sister back to life.

Hardaway Home, 1998

Candice was six when her baby sister, Brianna, came home from the hospital. She had waited patiently at the front window of their new home for what seemed like an eternity. Her knees burned and she had to pee, but she refused to move until she laid eyes on the newest member of the Hardaway clan.

It had only been two weeks since her father, Eric "Easy" Hardaway, had moved his family into a beautiful, new brownstone in the heart of Bed-Stuy, Brooklyn. Although their home address frequently changed, this was only the second move Candice could remember. The house was bigger and better than their last place. Even though Candice was young, she was fully aware that the new house and new car her father drove was more expensive than the last.

With her fists propped under her cheeks, Candice waited by the window until she spotted her father's sleek, large-bodied black Mercedes-Benz ease up to the curb in front of the house. Candice's mouth curled into a smile like someone had pulled up the corners with a crane—her dad affectionately referred to it as her "Joker" smile.

When her mother stepped out of the car, holding the tightly wrapped pink bundle in her arms, Candice felt her heart jerk in her chest. It was a mixture of excitement and fear. Until now, Candice had been the baby of the family, spoiled rotten by her father and overly protected by her brothers.

"Eric Junior! Errol! The baby is here!" Candice screeched, jumping off her knees, which were tattooed with an imprint of the couch's seams.

Her twin brothers were front and center in a matter of minutes.

The babysitter whom Easy had hired, a raven-haired girl named Lutisha, pulled back the door and Candice bolted outside.

"Let me see! Let me see the baby!" she panted, jumping into her father's arms so she could get a better look at the small body.

"Whoa, whoa, Candy Cane, let's get inside," Easy chuckled, his tone similar to a cowboy corralling an unruly horse.

Candice's mother, Corine, carried the baby up to the newly decorated nursery. Candice was hot on her heels.

"You're excited, huh?" Corine smiled softly at her daughter.

Candice nodded her head as she shifted her weight from one foot to the other.

Finally baby Brianna, who was wrapped up like a burrito, was unwrapped and introduced to Candice. Candice stood in awe. The baby's smell—a soft mixture of baby powder and Similac—made Candice want to never let her go. She loved the baby the minute she laid eyes on her. Brianna stared back, mutually infatuated.

The fanfare surrounding Brianna's birth didn't stop with Candice's obsessive attention, begging to hold her sister nearly every minute of the day. A week after coming home from the hospital, Easy and Corine planned the biggest welcome-to-the-world party for their newest addition. There was a huge pink-and-white cake, enough helium balloons to fill a small party hall and beautiful, poster-sized professional portraits of Brianna's first couple of days at home. Candice especially liked the picture with her holding Brianna alone.

Over seventy people attended the house party in honor of her baby sister. This made Candice feel somewhat envious; but even worse than that, there were no kids to play with. All of the attendees were adults and mostly friends of her father, along with their spouses or girlfriends. Candice found herself utterly bored.

Her father found her sitting in a corner with her arms folded. He walked over, his white teeth gleaming against his Hershey's chocolate–colored skin. "What's the long face for, Candy Cane?"

Candice ignored the questions and continued to pout.

"C'mon, Candy Cane, tell your favorite guy what's going on." Her father smiled.

"I don't want these people to touch my baby," Candice huffed, pushing her lip farther out.

Her father threw back his head, laughing. "Aw, Candy Cane, when everybody leaves, she'll be all yours again. I tell you what, why don't you go count all of the gifts in the front and I will make sure you get double the number of gifts for your birthday." He smiled and rumpled the top of her head.

Candice's eyes lit up. She knew her father always kept his promises.

"Okay! I'm going to stay there all night and count every gift!" she exclaimed, and ran toward the front foyer.

The gifts stacked on the floor near the front door were both large and small. Some were wrapped in pink paper, and some in pale green and yellow. Candice was careful and diligent in her job of counting the gifts as they arrived. She planned to remind her father of the deal he had made when her birthday came around.

As she stood at the front door, collecting and counting the gifts like a hired hostess/butler would, she noticed a man enter through the door without ringing the bell. He was a tall man with skin that made him look like a figure from the wax museum. The man's eyes resembled two black lumps of coal, and his hair was so dark and shiny that she couldn't help but stare at it.

"Hola, mamasita. Are you the hostess?" the man sang, bending down in front of her face.

He smiled and the shiny gold front left tooth nearly blinded her. Candice stared, mesmerized by the sparkly diamond skull and crossbones that was encrusted on the man's gold tooth. He looked like a dark pirate. Her mouth hung open and was filled with unladylike saliva.

"Is your Papa home?" the man asked her.

Before Candice could get her brain to connect with her tongue, she heard her father's voice interrupt her thoughts.

"Ayyy! I didn't expect to see you, boss," Easy said, his voice snapping her out of her trance.

Easy rushed toward the man and extended his hand; his face was plastered with feigned enthusiasm. Candice took note that her father seemed nervous; his speech was quicker and higher-pitched than usual. His normally relaxed mannerisms appeared tense. And no one made her father nervous.

"Easy, I wouldn't miss this for the world. We always take care of our own, and now you are one of our own," the man replied, inviting himself into the party room.

The way he spoke told Candice that he was like the man who owned the bodega at the corner of her block. The man who her mother always said was "Spanish," when Candice and her brothers laughed at the funny way the man spoke.

"But how did you know where I lived?" Easy asked, letting out a nervous chuckle.

"I know everything, amigo. *Not for you to worry, right? Now let me come in and see that new bundle of joy," the man replied, slapping Easy on the shoulder and shaking his hand roughly.*

Three men followed him inside the house. Candice was struck by the fact that, despite the warm and muggy weather outside, the men wore long leather trench coats, which were shiny and black like their hair. They all shared similar skin tones and eyes—like they weren't black, but they weren't white either. Candice did not like the way they looked or the way they talked. And she definitely didn't want anyone with a black leather coat or shiny gold tooth looking at or talking to her baby sister.

Still, she warily collected the boss's gifts and added it to her count. Candice lost interest in counting gifts after the "bad men" arrived. Candice couldn't stop sneaking a peek at the man and his three shadows.

Her mother also seemed not to be thrilled with the new party guests.

"Eric, I thought you told me you didn't get into the deal with the Dominicans. I don't like him. . . . He seems . . . very dangerous. Why would they come to something like this? To see a baby? How did they find where you live? They are trying to send a message, Eric. I don't like it." Her mother's tone was worried and on the verge of panic.

Candice watched as her father kissed her mother on the forehead.

"Corine, you worry too much. They just wanted to welcome the baby into the world," Easy said, but the creases in his forehead and the strain around his eyes told a different story.

Candice snapped out of her reverie and clicked play on her language CD. It was time to put things into motion. Step one was to embrace her new identity. The face of the man with the diamond-encrusted gold tooth was still plastered in her mind. Especially now, since the man seemed to be central to uncovering her father's secrets. Candice would never forget the man's face, but she just hoped he had forgotten hers.

Chapter 3

Untangling the Past

Junior sat on the leather couch in his upscale SoHo apartment as he stared across the small space at his mother. His mother slept peacefully on a custom-made circular bed, which Junior had imported from Italy a couple of years prior. Betty's Ambien-induced sleep was the norm for her lately.

Junior hadn't been to the apartment recently, but it was the only safe haven he had right now. When he originally rented the place, it served as his creep spot, a refuge from his boys and a place to take his women. Only a select few people knew about the apartment, and Junior was glad that he had heeded one of Easy's many street lessons: always keep a safe haven that nobody but you, and maybe your women, know about.

Junior thought about Easy a lot lately. Junior also wondered what Easy would do in his situation—the war with Phil and the uptown crew was far from over. Junior knew this, but it wasn't an ideal time to be thinking about killing people. Junior knew he couldn't just lie down and roll over—he had to fight and declare war, but it was all much easier said than done, especially given that his opponent was laying low and moving in silence and violence.

Junior had a lot of other things on his plate as well. He wondered what Easy would say about his daughter Candy trying to off him. Candy, who Junior had thought was a friend of Shana's, his brother's girl- friend, had threatened Junior's life; then he discovered that his right-hand man, Tuck, was an undercover DEA agent. Most shocking of all the revelations that day, however, was the old dude Rock's deathbed confession that he was, in fact, Junior's biological father.

As he rubbed his goatee, Junior sat and watched his mother sleep. His mind was racing with possibilities. His mind jumped from one thing to another. He was reminded of the many times he had come to his moth- er's rescue as a child. Junior was the one who helped his mother self-treat her wounds after her boyfriend would whip her ass, leaving her with busted lips and black eyes. Seeing her hurting back then and now made Junior feel helpless and threatened and ready to kill.

Junior kept replaying scenes from his past in his mind, and he grew angrier each time he remembered. Junior thought back to the first murder he'd commit- ted, and the irony that it was Easy who'd taken him un- der his wing and helped him out of that bad situation. Junior had suddenly been having a lot of memories of his life on the street with Easy.

Wortman Houses, 1988

Thirteen-year-old Junior stealthily walked up be- hind his mother's boyfriend like a quiet storm. Betty noticed him as she cowered in a corner, her body bent like a pretzel with her raised arms to shield off the next blow. Junior heard her suck in her breath at the sight of him. Sweat dripped down his brow and evil flashed in his eyes like he was of a demonic nature. Junior wore a wife beater, with his bony collarbone jutting out from the top, and a pair of jeans hung so low on his slim pelvis that the elastic band on his boxers was exposed. His eyes were hooded over with ill intent, and his mother could see fire flashing red in his wide pupils.

"Get ya hands off my mother, you punk-ass bitch!" Junior growled, baring his teeth like a hungry animal about to strike. His arms were extended out in front of him shaking fiercely, a combination of nerves and the weight of his newly acquired .22 special gripped tightly in his bony hands. "Slick! I said, get the fuck away from my mother!" Junior hissed again, his words firmer.

Slick was a tall, charcoal-colored man. He had a barrel chest and shoulders so wide that he resembled one of those ill-proportioned superhero action figures. He had been in and out of Betty's home for most of Junior's teenage years. Slick was his mother's current boyfriend who sometimes doubled as his baby brother Broady's father. Junior despised Slick from the first day he'd met him. When Slick started putting his hands on his mother, Junior's hate became palpable.

"Oh, you ain't hear me, bitch! I said, get ya fuckin' hands off my mother!" Junior barked again. This time he clicked his gun for emphasis.

Slick momentarily stopped beating his mother to peer at him, as one would a pestering insect.

"What, little punk? I know you ain't talkin' to me," Slick replied, turning to face Junior. His eyes went low at the sight of the gun in Junior's hands. "Whatchu gon' do with that?" Slick chortled incredulously. He faced Junior now, standing with his chest stuck out like a rooster about to go to battle over his hen.

"I'ma fuckin' shoot you, if you don't stop puttin' your hands on my mother!" Junior spat out, waving the gun in front of him.

"Oh yeah, go 'head and shoot me," Slick challenged, cracking the knuckles on his gorilla hands.

Betty scrambled to her feet and threw herself in front of Slick. "Stop it before somebody gets hurt! Junior, where did you get that thing? Put that gun down right now!" she demanded. Her voice had reached a high keening note.

"Move out the way, Ma. I'm not playin' with this bum-ass dude no more! I'm not sittin' in here, letting him punch on you no more!" Junior growled as sweat dripped into his left eye.

"I said put that thing down and get it out of my house!" Betty screeched unrelentingly.

"You gon' take up for him against your own son? I can't believe you! This no-good nigga be beating your ass! He don't give you no money! We starving around here! If I don't bring in food, we don't eat!" Junior screamed. His voice was cracking with hurt. The gun shook fiercely in his hands as his nerves got the better of him. Junior felt a sharp pain in his stomach; it was the gut punch of hurt feelings. His mother had chosen sides . . . again.

"Boy, you better listen to your mother before you end up in the Kings County morgue," Slick threatened, taking a stance behind Betty in case he needed a body shield.

"You' a punk-ass bastard hiding behind a woman," Junior spat. He looked at his mother with pure disdain and shook his head. "Stupid," he mumbled as he lowered his gun and turned on his heels and stomped into his room. Junior grabbed his newly purchased Polo leather-armed jacket and slid his feet into his newly purchased sneakers—all courtesy of his new job.

"Where you going?" Betty hollered at Junior's back, but all she heard in response was the slamming of a door.

Junior walked so fast down his block—he almost came out of his untied sneakers. His breath came out of his nose and mouth in strong, labored puffs, and his adrenaline coursed hot in his veins. Heading back to his spot on the block, Junior dared any crackhead or competing corner boy to try to test him today.

Just when he reached his usual post, he noticed Easy's car. "Shit," he cursed under his breath. Junior wasn't much in the mood for talking; and anytime he was around Easy, since the first day he'd started working for him, all Easy did was lecture Junior about the things he needed to be "smart" about.

Easy, of course, spotted him right away.

Easy was hanging with the old black dude again. "Ay! Why you lookin' like you wanna kill somebody?" Easy hollered out as he noticed Junior's high-yellow face flushed with anger.

The old dude eyed Junior up and down, sending an uncomfortable feeling over him.

"I almost just did!" Junior barked, sticking out his chicken chest like he was a big man.

"What? W'sup, kid?" Easy asked, placing his shoulder on Junior, steering him toward his car and away from the other corner boys in hearing distance.

Junior's chest was still rising and falling rapidly. He used his hand to swipe at the tears on his face and the snot running out of his nose.

"Who fucked with you kid?" Easy asked, his tone more serious. "You tell me if somebody is messing with you on these streets."

Junior looked into Easy's face and then over at the old dude, who was still standing a little ways away, acting like he wasn't listening. Something about the old dude seemed familiar to Junior, but he just couldn't place it.

"Nah, it's my mom's boyfriend. That dude be hittin' on her and I was gon' bust my piece in his ass just now, but she took up for his sorry ass, so I left," Junior explained.

Easy could relate. After all, he was Junior's age when he got fed up with an abusive male figure himself.

"What's his name?" Easy asked calmly, looking off into the distance.

"Slick, but his real name is Broady too, like my li'l brother."

"Where he be at?" Easy inquired, leaning back on the hood of his car, rubbing his hands together like a mad scientist concocting a diabolical plan.

"At that gambling spot behind Poppy's store. He be in there all day gambling away my mother's welfare check and his little piece of paycheck and any money we get in the house. That's why you seen me stealing the food that day you bought me the stuff from the store. . . . We don't have shit because of that nigga Slick. And my momz just keeps on taking him back in, like she dumb or sumthin'," Junior whined, jerking his head and shoulders with feeling.

Easy's gaze turned serious as he analyzed the situation.

"He's a fuckin' duck! I just wanna kill his ass!" Junior spat, shifting his weight from one foot to the other, itching for action.

"Calm down. Watch ya mouth! I'm still your elder. And stop letting all these jealous eyes out here on these streets see you upset and making threats. Niggas will turn state's witness on you in a New York minute," Easy warned. He nodded at the old dude, and the dude walked over.

"Seems like our little friend here got a problem he wanna take care of," Easy said to the old dude.

"This is my friend Rock . . . Mr. Rock to you, young-un," Easy introduced.

Junior remembered the man from the first day he met Easy, but he still didn't feel comfortable with the weird old dude, who always seemed to stare at him too long.

"Let's go pay your mom's boyfriend a visit in a bit. Just let me take care of what I came out here to do first. I'll be back to get you in a minute," Easy assured.

Junior breathed a sigh of relief. Easy seemed to have all the answers to his problems. He felt powerful around Easy, and he wanted to be just like him when he grew up.

Easy found Slick playing deep at one of the back tables in the smoky, underground gambling hole. He effortlessly kicked the legs of the folding chair Slick occupied, sending him toppling to the ground.

"Say sorry to the kid," Easy hissed, his dark boot pressed against Slick's neck. Slick knew who Easy was, and he wasted no time bitching out to his fear.

"Junior, li'l man . . . you know I be messing up sometimes, but—" Slick had started to speak, but his words were short-lived when the butt of Easy's gun landed on his skull, rendering him speechless.

"All I told you to say was sorry," Easy spat.

Slick's bladder involuntarily emptied on the floor of the basement gambling hole. The rest of the patrons of the illegal gambling spot had cleared out as soon as these intruders had arrived with their guns pointed and raised.

Junior felt powerful, like God right now. He was proud to be associated with Easy, and he loved seeing Slick humiliated.

"*Now try it again,*" *Easy instructed, forcing Slick's head up so he could look at Junior's face.*

"*Junior . . . little man,*" *Slick said.*

His words caused Mr. Rock to flinch.

"*Don't call me that,*" *Junior gritted.* "*I'm not none of your li'l man. You don't be acting all nice when you tryin'a kick my mom's ass, nigga!*" *Junior spat out.*

"*I—I'm sorry, man. I love Betty. You gotta believe me. I . . . can't control it sometimes,*" *Slick pleaded.*

Watching his grown ass start to cry like a bitch was a shameful sight to see.

"*You a sorry-ass bitch. You always sayin' sorry, but you go right back to doing it,*" *Junior accused. Mr. Rock whispered something to Easy.*

"*This is taking too long, Junior. It's time for you to get your feet wet. You always face your enemies and let them see your eyes before you engage in warfare,*" *Easy told him.*

Junior looked Slick in the eyes. He leveled his gun at his chest and pulled the trigger. Junior's body stumbled backward from the powerful shot. He dropped the gun like it was a piece of hot coal.

Slick's body slumped to the floor.

Junior stood stock-still; his eyes were as wide as saucers, and his body trembling.

Easy grabbed him by the shoulders before he collapsed to the floor.

"*Let's go. You a man now,*" *Easy declared as he led Junior away from the murder scene. Easy stopped him for a minute and looked at him seriously.* "*You only ever kill people that are a threat to you or your family, and you never get back at a man through his woman or children,*" *Easy sternly lectured. Junior nodded his agreement.* "*I learned that from him,*" *Easy said, nodding toward Rock.*

Word on the street the next day was that Slick was killed in a gambling spot over a bad debt.

Junior was now reminded of just how powerful he felt the day he took a man's life. The thought compelled him into action. Junior picked up his cell phone and dialed a number.

"Hey, it's Junior. I need a meeting. This *is* fucking life or death," Junior spat. After hanging up the phone, he walked over and touched his mother's cheek. She moved slightly but was still knocked out.

"I didn't let anyone hurt you then, and I'm damn sure not going to let them do it now," he promised before leaving the apartment.

Chapter 4

Sorting Out The Truth

Avon took the long way to Dana Carlisle's house. As he pulled up, he could see Carlisle peeking through her front blinds. He smirked when she pulled the door back before he could even lift his fist to knock.

"Come in," Carlisle greeted. Tucker walked inside just like he had for the past three weeks of crashing at Dana's place.

"Look, Dana . . . about the way I acted. . . ," he started to apologize. He had argued with her the day before. Tucker had grown frustrated when Carlisle insisted that she would help him find information on Candy and Easy Hardaway. Tucker had told her it was too risky, but she had insisted on helping him. She had never seen him so passionate about a case. He had also never seen her so hell-bent on getting involved in one.

"Shh. I understand. You were just trying to protect an old friend," Carlisle joked, winking at him. She gave him a thorough once-over. Avon had stayed at a hotel after their argument. He looked like he had shit, showered and shaved. She stared at him, starstruck by all his sexiness.

"I can't stay long. I have a lot of things to get straight in my life," Tucker explained, taking a seat on Carlisle's futon, which had served as his bed when he stayed with her.

"I understand," she whispered. "Are you finally going to try to go home? You know . . . work things out with her?" she asked, trying to sound nonchalant. In reality, the green-eyed monster of jealousy was slowly crawling up her back.

"You said you had something important to show me, right?" Tucker got straight to the point. She had called him with an urgency to come by. He figured it would be something related to Candy.

"Yeah, I do." Carlisle conceded his abrupt shift in subject, knowing that she had struck a nerve. She rushed into her home office, talking over her shoulder. "So you must be glad to be in one piece after all you went through," Carlisle called out, her voice growing faint as she walked to the back of her house.

"Yeah. It's all been really crazy. Look . . . let's not . . ." Tucker replied evasively. He had already told her he couldn't involve her.

Carlisle shuffled back into the living room, dragging a large box behind her. Tucker offered his assistance by casually brushing her hands away and lifting the box onto the pub-style dinette set in her kitchen.

"Well, this is what I wanted to give you. Don't say I've never given you any gifts," Carlisle said flirtatiously.

"What exactly is all of this?" Tucker asked, surveying the large, dusty box.

"It's all the shit you need to know, all packaged up. It's also the thing that could get me fired from the DEA, and probably earn me the top spot on somebody's fuckin' hit list, so guard that stuff with your life. I don't really understand everything, even after I read through most of this stuff. But it seems like after the Hardaway family was killed, the DEA tossed the house and found what's in the box. I couldn't really believe it myself. Never thought I'd ever see the day when a drug dealer would be writing down his life story," Dana said, shaking her head.

Avon looked at her strangely.

"Yeah, that's the same reaction I had when I saw what was in those boxes," Dana told him. "I'm telling you, the shit reads just like a fiction novel, Tuck. Eric Hardaway was in deep. You have to read this shit for yourself," Carlisle huffed, placing her hands on her hips.

"Where'd you find—" Avon started to say.

"Don't ask me any questions. You didn't want me to ask you any, and I don't want you to ask me any. Just take it and make good use of it," she said, smiling wanly.

Tucker had no idea just how desperate she had been to help him get the information he sought. Or the depraved acts she had performed to gather these documents. She owed more than a few people in the classified archives a bunch of favors.

"Thanks for this and for everything else. I'm sorry I can't . . . I never intended to . . ." Tucker was stumbling, truly tongue-tied. He never meant to drag her into the mix. All he'd wanted to do in the first place was go undercover, make a big bust and then redeem himself.

Dana shifted her weight from one foot to the other and shoved her restless hands into the back pockets of her jeans. Avon was clearly having a difficult time saying the words that were in his mind, but not on his tongue: *I'm sorry I kind of used you, although I know I could never be attracted to you, because I am in love with someone else.*

Things between them had happened so fast. The revelations that Brubaker was trying to set him up to look like a rogue agent; watching Rock Barton shoot himself in the femoral artery. Watching Candy suffer as she learned that her own brother, under the government's direction, had killed her father. It was enough to make anyone go crazy.

Carlisle had been there at the end. Her smiling, loyal face was the only comfort in the face of death, destruction and betrayal. Dana had opened up her arms and her home to Avon, listening to him pour out his heart over his wife, over Candy and over his time on the street.

In the end her porcelain skin and the lemony smell of her shampoo had made him feel clean and whole. She'd rubbed his bald head and massaged the tension out of his neck. Her long, spindly fingers kneaded him, probing him.

Their first kiss was electric. It was hot, fast and furious. Animalistic.

He'd devoured her tongue like a starving refugee. She nearly ripped his shirt from his muscular chest. Her mouth moved over him so fast—he felt like she'd set his chest ablaze.

Carlisle had made the first move by removing her jeans and then her panties to expose her woman's core. Tuck felt flush; his body betrayed him. His emotions were on overload and he mindlessly took her: forcefully, brutally, clenching his ass cheeks with every release of his hurt, frustrated loneliness.

She had screamed out more than once—mostly from pleasure, not pain—but she certainly could not have enjoyed their coupling very much.

He had been brutal and selfish and completely insensitive to her wants and needs. After ejaculating, he had collapsed on the futon, spent.

The next day, neither spoke about the events that had transpired in the dark. Instead, the focus had switched back to Avon's impending task—finding Candy.

Shaking away the memory—the mistake—Avon finally decided he would just let the heavy silence that stood between them remain intact, like the Great Wall of China.

"You okay?" Carlisle asked, noticing his glassy, blank stare.

"Oh . . . yeah. I'm—I'm just gonna go," he said, stumbling, his palms sweaty. He leaned toward her awkwardly, giving her a clumsy hug.

Carlisle felt light-headed and unsteady on her feet. She lifted her arms uncomfortably and pat his back—a friendly pat like what men would exchange. She fought the urge to kiss him on the neck. She inhaled his scent and closed her eyes. She was glad that she could help him unravel the Hardaway case. In the meantime, she planned to keep a close eye on him—whether he liked it or not.

Avon got into his car and stared over at the box he had placed on the passenger seat. His first thought was to drive to a safe place and look inside, but the anxious feeling in the pit of his stomach prevented him from moving. The dark-tinted windows on the car gave him a sense of security that no one would be able to see inside. He finally gave in to his curiosity and pulled back the thick gray duct tape sealing the box.

The first notebook on the pile was an old-school black-and-white marble composition book. Tucker picked it up and read the cover: MY LIFE, BY ERIC HARDAWAY. Pressed for answers that might lead him to learn more about the young girl he'd become so obsessed with, Avon placed the old dusty notebook against the steering wheel and began to read. Just like Carlisle had said, it was like reading a book.

Avon immediately escaped into the life of Easy Hardaway.

Brooklyn, New York, 1983

"You little bastard! Get ya ass over here!" Doobey screamed, his pale face turning crimson.

Eric stood rooted to the floor. His fists were balled at his side. His chest was rising and falling rapidly. He wasn't going that easily this time.

"Did you hear me?" Doobey barked, stepping closer to his nephew.

Eric squinted his eyes into little dashes and folded his face into a scowl.

"Oh, you gon' stand there like you that fuckin' man! You s'pose to scare me? I'ma show you who the man is in this muthafucka!" Doobey spat out. Small sprinkles of his Colt 45–scented spittle landed on Eric's face.

Still, Eric refused to move while his drunken uncle struggled to get his cowhide belt off his pants.

This type of commotion was commonplace in his Aunt Deena's house; so much so, that his cousins didn't even bother to intervene. They simply exited the room as soon as the altercation took place. Deena never intervened when her husband beat the shit out of her nephew; in fact, in Eric's assessment, his aunt encouraged it.

Deena was his mother's sister. She had seven children of her own—all cramped into a two-bedroom apartment—so she resented the fact that she had to care for her sister's orphaned child.

Easy's mother, Cynthia, was one of the first female drug dealers in Brooklyn. His father, Erv, had turned Cynthia on to the game. They were an unstoppable duo, until jealous rival dealers executed them both.

Immediately after their deaths, Easy went to live with his grandmother, who died of a broken heart, he believed, shortly after his mother's murder.

Then he moved in with his maternal aunt, where he was reminded daily that he was unwanted and unloved.

"Now! I said get the fuck over here, boy!" Doobey growled, finally getting his belt free.

Eric looked at him evilly. "Fuck you! You ain't my father!" Eric hissed, clenching his fists so tightly that his nails dug half-moon–shaped craters into his palms.

"After this ass whupping you gon' wish I was ya daddy!" Doobey slurred, raising the belt over his shoulder.

Eric felt a hot rush of adrenaline come over his body. Moved by some unknown force, he lifted his left fist. When Doobey went to plow into him, Eric punched his uncle in the balls with all of the strength he could muster.

Eric growled as his unsuspecting uncle doubled over in pain. It was a bold move; but like an animal trapped in a corner, Eric felt his only choice was to attack. He started swinging wildly, landing punches at will on Doobey's head, face and chest.

With his equilibrium off from drinking, Doobey tried to stop Eric's wild blows, but he couldn't see straight enough to grab the ferocious fists flying at him.

"I hate you!" Eric screamed, throwing more punches and kicks. He finally tackled his uncle to the floor; he sat on his chest and lit into him.

"*Get him off me!*" *Doobey gasped, the combination of alcohol and head injuries making him feel nauseated and dizzy.*

Eric was like a machine that could not be turned off. He thought about all of the nights his uncle had come home, stinking drunk, and beat him out of his sleep just because he could. All of the times his uncle took his dinner plate, forcing him to go to bed with his insides churning from hunger. He thought about all of the times his grandmother allowed his cousins to tease him about his raggedy sneakers and clothes.

As if possessed by the devil himself, Eric felt spit fly out of his mouth, and tears ran down his cheeks. For the first time in his life, he felt an overwhelming sense of power over his life. He felt invincible, strong enough to kill his uncle with his bare hands.

Blood leaked out of his uncle's nose by the time Deena shuffled her obese body into the cramped living room and tried to pull her lunatic nephew off her drunken husband.

"Boy! You ain't gon' be hittin' on my man! You need to get the hell out of my house!" Deena hollered as she tried in vain to pull Eric off Doobey. A crowd of cousins surrounded the two tangled bodies and moved in like vultures over a dead carcass.

"Get the fuck off me! I hate y'all! I hate all of y'all!" Eric screamed, kicking and flailing, as his eldest cousin, Poopie, finally pulled his arms behind his back. "I hate this house!" Eric screeched.

Turning to Deena, he eyed his aunt with all of the hate he'd augmented over the years. "This is all your fault! You evil bitch! You just jealous because my mother had everything and you ain't got shit!" he growled, pushing his aunt in the chest.

"Oh, God!" she implored, clutching her chest as she stumbled backward into a beat-up armchair. She had just narrowly missed hitting the floor.

"Uh-nuh! No, he didn't!" Screams erupted all around Eric and the entire house reacted, thirsty for his blood.

"You ain't gon' be hitting my mother!" one of his less courageous cousins barked from a distance.

There was no telling what Eric would do next. In a matter of seconds, the group converged as one large avenging angel. Blows started to land on Eric's body. Somebody dragged him down to the floor and kicked him sharply in his kidneys. His breath escaped painfully, but he refused to show any other signs of weakness. Another blow to the top of his head made him see small streams of squirming lights behind his eye sockets.

There was no way he could win against all of his cousins. Scrambling on the floor, trying to protect his head, Eric finally made it to the door.

"Let him up! He wanna leave. Let the bastard leave!" Deena shouted, her face filling with blood and her double chin jiggling.

Eric snatched the door open and ran out of the apartment. His nose was bleeding; his left eye was nearly swollen shut. His knuckles were raw, and he felt like he had broken a few ribs.

Slamming the door shut behind him, Eric realized that he was walking away from the only family he had ever known. But not all families, in his estimation, were worth holding on to. He had survived all these years, and he would survive many more. At just thirteen years old, he may have been homeless, but he wasn't hopeless.

The first night his aunt kicked him out, Eric sat in a dark, dank space behind the stairs of the apart-

ment building, nodding in and out of sleep. When he emerged from his hiding spot the next morning, his insides were churning from hunger. His body ached and his left eye was black and swollen shut.

Eric walked three blocks to the corner store, praying that he wouldn't run into any of his cousins. His plan was to sneak in the back of the store, grab a few bags of chips, to kill the hunger pains tearing out his insides, and then dip back out, unseen. He had been psyching himself up all the way to the store. He had never stolen anything in his life. As he turned the corner, he heard shouting and screaming. He remained hidden behind a large dumpster, silently watching two men punch, kick and stomp on the body of a man who lay on the ground, screaming and squirming.

Eric had never heard a man scream like a woman before. He kept his eyes glued to the scene, but something in his peripheral vision caught his attention.

A long, darkly tinted 1975 black Cadillac Sedan Deville, with whitewash wheels, sat parked in front of the store. The back window was halfway down and Eric could see the face of a man watching the brawl. The man wore a dark brown suede fedora with a red feather attached at the side. His face was the color of molasses, and a mustache covered his top lip with thick, coarse black hair.

Eric turned his eyes from the man in the car back to the victim, who had stopped squirming and screaming. Judging from the amount of blood pooling on the ground around the man's head, Eric decided that the man was probably dead.

"That's enough!" the man in the Cadillac yelled out the window, snapping his fingers. Like well-trained dogs in obedience school, the men stopped beating the limp, lifeless man.

"You, kid! C'mere," the fedora-clad man called out to Eric.

Eric's mouth hung open, and he frantically looked around, hoping that there was another kid nearby whom he was beckoning. When the man pointed his finger directly at him, Eric nearly peed his pants.

"Me?" he croaked in fear.

"Listen, little brotha, don't play with me. You don't see nobody else out here at six o'clock in the damn morning, do you? Now, I said, c'mere," the man snapped.

Eric walked over like a man on his way to the gas chamber. His legs felt like lead pipes, and the hunger pangs in his stomach were replaced by doom-filled cramps.

The man who had summoned him reached his hand out the window toward Eric. Eric immediately took notice of the huge yellow-gold and diamond ring on the man's pinkie. The man grabbed the collar of Eric's shirt and pulled him up to the side of the car so that the metal door frame pushed into his chest.

The man moved his face a mere two inches from Eric's. *"You see that jive-ass bitch over there on the ground?"* the man asked.

With his one good eye stretched wide to its limit, Eric moved his head up and down in concurrence.

"Well, he got what he deserved for being a bitch. Ain't nothin' worse than a man who acts like a bitch. Don't you agree?"

Eric nodded his head up and down rapidly.

"All right, then. If you tell anybody who you saw giving that bitch what he deserved, that same thing gon' happen to you. 'Cause if you tell, that would make you a rat bitch, now wouldn't it? You feel me? Look like somebody done worked yo' ass over, anyhow," the man ground out, looking at Eric with squinted eyes.

Eric moved his head up and down. The man finally released his grip on Eric's collar.

"What's your name, boy?" he asked, softening his tone. There was something about Eric that he liked—an innocence he could fuck with.

"Er . . . um . . . Eric."

"Well, I'm Early. Ask anybody roun' here about me if you don't believe what I'm telling you 'bout what can happen to you," the man warned. "Now, if the police ask you what you saw here, what you gon' say?" Early asked.

"I'ma say I ain't s—see nothin'," Eric stammered. His tongue felt thick and heavy in his mouth.

"See . . . you wrong already. Whatcha gonna say is that you saw some young boys robbing that dude right there and they beat him up till he stopped movin'."

Eric nodded in agreement. "Yeah . . . that's what I'ma say."

"Good," Early replied with a half smile, half sneer. He was going to have fun with this young man.

He gave Eric a once-over. "Why you out here so early in the damn morning, anyway? School don't be starting till another two hours or so." Early chuckled. He hadn't been in a school building in nearly two decades.

"Um . . . I . . . I . . ." Eric was scared to tell the man the true reason for his vagrancy.

"Don't think about lying to me, boy. I can find out anything I wanna know about these streets. Now I see somebody don' kicked yo ass around, and you look hungry and thirsty with those crusty white-ass lips. You best tell me what's goin' on," Early demanded.

Eric hung his head low; he didn't even know where to start. Instead of coming up with a good story, Eric decided that the truth would be easier to tell.

When he had finished his tale, he was surprised to find Early in deep thought. The man twirled one end of his mustache, as if contemplating the meaning of the universe itself. Suddenly he stopped, looked at Eric, opened his Cadillac door and said, "Get in. I think you need a job, young-un. And a good street name to go with it. You seem real easygoing kid, so I'm gon' call you Easy."

Eric cracked a nervous smile. "Easy . . . I like that name."

Early took his young new protégé to McDonald's to fill his empty belly and then to the shopping mall to buy some new clothes. After a shower and a few hours of sleep, Eric felt like a new person. Early took Easy under his tutelage and they formed a quick bond. Easy didn't really have a choice in the matter. Early promised to protect him, and he did just that.

"Punch this punk bitch one more time," Early instructed, twirling the end of his mustache nonchalantly. Easy did as he was told. He pulled back his fist and laid it into his uncle Doobey's lower abdomen one more time.

"Aggh," Doobey coughed. Early laughed.

"You ain't so tough now, are you?" Early hawked up a mucus-filled wad of spit and spewed it into the center of Doobey's face. "I ain't got no respect for a bitch-ass man who puts his hands on a helpless kid," Early observed as his follow-up.

Easy looked on as one of Early's henchmen kicked Doobey square in the balls. His aunt would definitely not be producing any more children in the years to come. Watching Doobey double over in excruciating pain gave Easy a sense of satisfaction that he'd never felt before. Revenge felt like a drug he could indulge in often.

The beating continued for what seemed like an eternity. "I'm sick of looking at this chump-ass pussy. Take his ass outta my sight," Early instructed.

His workers hoisted Doobey's badly battered body from the floor. They stopped in front of Easy. Early walked over and grabbed a handful of Doobey's Afro and lifted up his head.

"Say sorry to this fuckin' kid," Early instructed.

Doobey moaned. His lips were so swollen that Easy couldn't even understand his words.

"Did you hear him say 'sorry'?" Early asked Easy.

Easy nodded his head up and down. He didn't think he was ready to watch someone he knew die.

Easy never saw Doobey or any of his family members after that day. He worked for Early, and in his Brooklyn neighborhood that meant something. Nobody fucked with him anymore; in fact, he was gaining a lot of respect around his way.

Easy's job was to pick up packages from a Spanish dude in the Bronx and bring the goods back to Early. Early paid Easy $100 for each delivery, which was more money than Easy had ever seen in his life. He grew to love the feel and the smell of money, and the freedom it could buy him. With Early's generous paychecks, Easy bought his own clothes, his own food and anything else that he desired. Early even provided a roof over Easy's head by offering him a cot to sleep on in the small living space in the back of his pool hall.

Easy quickly became known at the hangout spot and all around the neighborhood as "Early's kid." Easy liked being claimed by someone; it made him feel wanted. He looked up to Early, and he wanted to be just like him.

Easy would stand in the tiny pool hall bathroom and practice walking, talking and looking like Early.

Over the years Early would kick little jewels of knowledge to Easy, like telling him to never, ever trust a man who couldn't look him in the eye.

"If a man can't look you straight in the eye," Early lectured, "the man is hiding his real self."

Early had even gotten Easy his first piece of ass. The advice that followed was invaluable.

"Never fall in love with your first," Early had lectured. "If you do, you'll never have shit to compare it with, so you'll never know what you're missing out on."

Tuck wondered how much Candy knew about her father's upbringing. There was so much more to Eric Hardaway than met the eye, and so many loose ends that needed tying up.

Chapter 5

Deal with the Devil

Candice followed the small Hispanic woman with her eyes. The petite, raven-haired woman balanced a chubby-faced baby on one hip and held the hand of a little boy who looked to be preschool age. The woman released the little boy's hand for a quick second while she struggled to open the door of the sleek black hybrid vehicle. As soon as she released the boy's hand, he took off running like a prison escapee.

Candice was able to see his face clearly now. The family resemblance was stark, with classic olive-toned skin and slanted dark eyes. The boy's shiny black hair bounced around his perfectly round face as his arms pumped with each stride of his run. The woman looked frantic as she took off after the little rascal, the weight of the baby on her hip slowing her down. Candice held her breath as she watched the show unfold.

"Rolando! Come back! Rolando, please!" the woman called out, clearly exasperated.

Candice slid farther down into her seat as the boy, named after his grandfather, ran straight in the direction of her car.

"Rolando! *Por favor!*" the woman huffed pleadingly; the baby was bouncing precariously in her arms. With an outstretched arm the nanny caught a handful of fabric from the back of his shirt and twisted him around.

She spoke rapidly in Spanish; her raised eyebrows, twisted lips and tight hold on the boy indicated a severe scolding was ensuing.

Candice let out a long sigh of relief that the woman had caught the boy just before he neared her vehicle. It might not have gone over so well if the woman had noticed Candice sitting in a car with dark shades covering her eyes, watching them. This was the second week Candice had spent observing them.

Every Thursday, at eleven-thirty in the morning, the nanny took the children to the park. Candice was surprised that such a notorious family as the DeSosas would allow their nanny or any member of the family, for that matter, to be in such a strict routine. Didn't they worry that their enemies could be watching?

Candice thought the DeSosa grandchildren would be chauffeured around in grand limousines by huge, strapping bodyguards with dark shades covering their eyes.

Some notorious drug kingpin, she thought. *Maybe my father was the only paranoid drug kingpin to ever live?*

Either way, DeSosa's slipup worked in her favor.

Once the woman secured the kids into their respective car seats, Candice started her ignition. She had to be at the ready. Keeping a safe distance behind, Candice followed the vehicle to the beautiful Saddlebrook, New Jersey, home.

Just last week Candice had followed the nanny inside Starbucks to study her target at closer range.

"Hey, Flora . . . you want your usual light caramel macchiato?" The barista smiled.

Hard Candy 2: Secrets Uncovered

Flora.

It was amazing how much she could find out about a person, even by something as simple as following her into a coffee shop. Candice knew she could take Flora out with no problem. One pressure point stun and the little woman could be easily incapacitated. Candice had kept that in mind.

Lucky for Flora and DeSosa, Candice lived by her father's creed—no women and children. The lesson had obviously been lost on DeSosa when he decided that her mother and eight-year-old sister were fair game.

However, a little manipulation and deception were needed to accomplish what Candy envisioned, and that entailed using women and children as a means to an end. So long as no women or children were physically harmed, Candy felt she could live with the consequences.

The following day, Candice took a different route to the city. She already knew the nanny was heading to the petting zoo at Central Park, but not before she would pull up to the Starbucks just outside of the park to grab her light caramel macchiato. She consistently left both children in the idling car.

Candice was already parked across the street from the Starbucks when the familiar black hybrid pulled up. "Like clockwork," Candice whispered, an involuntary smirk spreading across her lips. She watched Flora get out, run around the back of the car and rush into the Starbucks.

Go! Candice prompted herself. She scrambled out of her car, raced across the street, crouched down on the side of the car that was facing the street, and used a gloved hand to open the vehicle's back door.

Little Rolando sat up and looked at her, his little head tilted curiously. His baby sister was sound asleep.

"Shh," Candice whispered, placing her finger up to her lips. "Rolando, you wanna see a doggy?" Candice reached inside and unfastened his car seat strap. The boy still looked at her strangely; then he smiled and nodded his agreement.

Rolando wasted no time showing that he was a big boy, happy to be free from the captivity of his car seat. He hopped out of the seat and took Candy's proffered hand. She closed the door, careful not to wake the baby.

"C'mon, let's go see the doggy," she announced. She lifted him between two parked cars and put him on the sidewalk. "Go, look at the doggy over there," she said, pointing to a dog-grooming service two doors down that had their latest customers on display in the window. "Go ahead, big boy," Candice urged when he hesitated. She patted him on the bottom; then she looked around, making sure she didn't draw too much attention to herself or to the boy.

As expected, Rolando took off running.

Candice watched him for a few seconds, keeping her body low. She peeped at the Starbucks and saw that Flora was already coming toward the door with her drink. A flash of heat engulfed Candice's chest. She was spurred into action. She turned quickly, but she couldn't dart across the street just yet. The Manhattan traffic was whizzing by.

"Shit!" Candice huffed, jumping back. Breathing hard and tapping her foot, Candice waited, eyeing the car. Flora was inside now.

Finally there was a break in traffic. With her heart hammering wildly, Candice sprinted back across the street, hoping the woman hadn't noticed her next to the car. With her chest rising and falling rapidly, and her nostrils wide, Candice slumped back into her car. Once inside, she let out a long sigh of relief.

Candice glanced at the black hybrid and noticed Flora standing beside it with a look of terror etched on her face. Her hands were up in the air, swaying wildly, and her head whipped left and right in a frantic motion. She looked to be on the verge of screaming or fainting. Candice lowered her window slowly so she could hear the commotion more clearly.

"Help! *Por favor!* Help!" Flora screamed, her voice a grating, high-pitched call of distress. Flora yanked open the backseat door and snatched the crying infant to her side as if afraid that she would disappear as well. "Help me!" she screamed again at the top of her lungs. People began to stop and look. Some Good Samaritans offered to dial 911, while others tried to calm her down. Flora continued to whirl around; hysteria was setting in now.

Sirens blared in the distance. Candice knew the boy's exact whereabouts. He had done more than just look at the dogs in the shop's window. When a dog owner had exited, he quickly slipped into the grooming store, which fit beautifully into Candice's plans. A warm sense of satisfaction rose from her stomach into her heart.

Flora was sitting down in the driver's seat of the vehicle; her feet and legs were hanging out the door. The baby was perched on her lap, and the crowd of Good Samaritans was around her, anxious for the authorities to arrive. A few of them volunteered to look for the little boy and they spread out across the block, calling out "Rolando."

Candice knew that it was only a matter of time before the boy was found in the pet shop.

Four police cars, with flashing blue and red lights, arrived at the scene, parking haphazardly around the vehicle. Two officers questioned Flora; two spoke to the bystanders; the rest of the officers began a methodical grid search.

Candice had to chuckle a bit. The boy was right under their noses. The police began checking the stores almost immediately, just as Candice predicted. The officers who would find the boy would be dubbed heroes back at the station for reuniting the lost child with his nanny.

This incident would be the first of many tragedies that would befall the DeSosa family in the coming weeks, if Candy had anything to do with it.

Shortly after the cops arrived, a white Range Rover came to screeching halt near the police cars. Arellio DeSosa, whom Candice recognized from her photo collage, was out of his car before it even came to a full stop. Rolando DeSosa's eldest son burst through the throngs of onlookers and officers and headed straight for Flora. His body language was rigid and menacing.

Before Arellio could even utter a harsh word, a petite blonde, with a lithe build, rushed from behind him. Her hands were extended in front of her as if ready to scratch Flora's eyes out.

"You bitch! Where is my son?" the blonde screamed.

Candice slouched down even farther in her seat and smiled. She'd finally gotten to see Arellio's wife. A police officer grabbed the woman's arms behind her back and directed her toward the Range Rover before she could do any real harm to the nanny. The woman's hands and mouth were moving a mile a minute.

Arellio scolded Flora, his finger wagging accusatorily in her face. Snatching his daughter from her arms, he headed back toward his wife.

"You're fuckin' fired!" the blonde screeched, trying to outmaneuver the officer. "Where is my son?" The woman broke down, her shoulders shaking, as she covered her face with her hands.

Flora was sobbing as well. She had always been careful. There was no way the boy could've unfastened his own car seat straps. The thought caused Flora's knees to give out. She almost hit the ground before an officer caught her in his arms.

Candice watched intently as Arellio handed his daughter to his wife and engaged in an intense conversation with the police officers. Candice watched him still trying to be the cool kingpin as the pressure mounted. Candice hated him more and more by the minute. She made her hand into a fake gun. Closing her weak eye, she aimed it at Arellio's head.

"Boom!" she whispered as she pulled back her pointer finger in a mock trigger pull.

Arellio went over and embraced his wife; their baby daughter was snuggled between them.

Such a loving family, Candice noted sarcastically.

Alas, the play was nearing its final scene. Heads turned simultaneously to the left as shouting could be heard in the distance.

"Found him! We found him!" a police officer belted out as he walked with a child in his arms toward the crowd. Cheers erupted from the worried onlookers.

Arellio and wife rushed toward their child. "Thank God!" the woman cried as she scooped her son up into her arms and squeezed him tightly. Arellio was right on her heels. He kissed his son on the top of his head and held on to his wife and children for dear life.

The scene sent sparks of white-hot anger over Candice's body. Her cheeks were aflame and she bit down so hard into the side of her mouth that she broke the skin.

"Now I know how to locate your Achilles' heel," Candice vowed aloud as she followed Arellio DeSosa with her eyes. Family clearly mattered to him, as much as it did to her. If that was his point of weakness, then that was where she planned to strike first.

Standing nearly six and a half feet tall, Arellio DeSosa was a hard-to-miss target. He was nearly the spitting image of his father—olive-colored skin, shiny black hair, strong broad shoulders, large flat nose and long prominent chin. He joined his father's business when he was just seventeen years old and was groomed to be just as ruthless. Unlike most teenage boys, however, Arellio's rite of passage into manhood was murder.

Harlem, New York 1991

As a .357 Magnum shook in Arellio's hand, his father and his goons waited for the young protégé to find the cojones to finish the job.

"There is no hesitation, Arellio!" Rolando DeSosa barked.

Arellio jumped at the sound of his father's voice. He had always been scared of his father, who was very much an authoritative figure in his life.

"When a man betrays you, your family, everything you stand for, you have no choice but to kill him—no matter who he is. There is no coming back for a man who has no dignity and no pride," DeSosa lectured his son.

"This man stole from me. He lied to my face! He threatened our family by talking to the police. He is a snake . . . no, more like a fuckin' rat," DeSosa hissed, his accent strengthening.

Arellio looked down at the bloodied man whom he'd once called Uncle. The man squirmed on the floor in a last-ditch effort to edge toward the door and save his life; he really did look like a slithering snake.

Arellio followed him now, leveling his gun at his chest. He couldn't breathe. His heart beat so fast—he thought he'd go into cardiac arrest.

"What are you waiting for? He is no longer part of our family. He betrayed me, our family name and everything we stand for." DeSosa was urging his son to finish the job. He needed to know that Arellio had the heart to kill. It was the only way he could guarantee his family's reputation as cold-blooded businessmen.

"This is your chance to live up to the DeSosa name. You must not feel anything for a rat bastard like this. Now, prove to me, and everyone here, that you're worthy of this family's name," DeSosa growled. He was growing frustrated with his son's apparent hesitation.

With his body covered in a cold sweat, Arellio lifted his gun hand and aimed it at the man's head. His uncle flipped onto his back. He looked into his nephew's eyes, pleading for a small measure of compassion.

"Please, please . . ." the man's voice quavered. "Your mother is my sister. What will she think when she finds out I'm dead at your hands? You can't devastate her like this. You're just a young boy. You don't understand what is going on here," the man cried out, his words barely audible through swollen lips.

Arellio gazed at the men gathered in the room to witness his first kill. He couldn't disappoint his father in front of all of his workers. Arellio had to prove that he was worthy of the family business and of his father's love. This was his chance.

"Shut up! Don't talk about my mother!" Arellio shouted. "You are a fuckin' rat bastard, just like my father said!" Arellio could nearly feel the testosterone flowing in his veins. He got closer to the man and put the gun to the man's temple.

"You must die," he announced to his uncle. He closed his eyes and pulled the trigger before he could have any second thoughts.

The gun blast reverberated up Arellio's arm and caused his body to rock backward. When he opened his eyes, he saw part of the man's brains lying on the floor. There was so much blood. Arellio felt his knees go weak. Blood and brain matter had splattered all over his shoes and the bottom of his pants.

Taking the man's life made him feel as powerful as God Himself. He gripped the gun more tightly now. He looked around wildly. His eyes darted from face to face. He locked eyes with his father. Arellio bit down into his jaw and tried not to crack a smile. Instead, he adjusted his features into a scowl, as was appropriate for a murdering man.

"Good job, my son. I knew you could do it," DeSosa said proudly as he clapped his son on the shoulder.

Arellio could not stop staring at his handiwork. The smell of the blood, like raw meat gone bad, made him feel like an animal in the jungle prowling for his next meal. Only Arellio didn't think this particular appetite could ever be truly satisfied.

Junior sat across from Rolando DeSosa Sr. Their eyes were locked on each other. DeSosa lifted a Cuban cigar to his lips slowly, sucking in, and blew a smoke ring in Junior's direction. His infamous diamond skull and crossbones gleamed on his front tooth. Junior bit down into his jaw and adjusted his neck.

"Junior," DeSosa drawled, rolling the *R* at the end of his name.

Junior didn't break eye contact.

"You come here for my help, no?" DeSosa said in an unnervingly calm tone of voice.

Junior nodded slightly.

"But you question me also?" DeSosa followed up. He didn't appreciate the way Junior had accused him with fingers pointed.

"Look, DeSosa, I'm sorry for the way I busted in here. I'm just telling you what this dude said. First he said you worked for the government, and then he said he was a fuckin' DEA agent," Junior confessed as he recalled the nightmarish scene that had unfolded weeks earlier.

On that night Junior had discovered that his right-hand man, Tuck, was really an undercover DEA agent. "I had no idea. I feel like my ass had been set up by you, by him. . . . I just want some answers, man. I also want help with this problem," Junior continued, humbly now. He was very careful with his tone as he warily eyed DeSosa's goons positioned on either corner of the room. Another was stationed on the other side of the closed door.

DeSosa moved his shoulders back uncomfortably. "You came here for my help? You say Phil harmed your family? Is that right?" DeSosa asked, blowing out more smoke rings. He completely ignored Junior's concerns about him being down with the government.

Junior nodded, rocking in his chair now. His frustration was mounting.

"And what about his brother? His family?" DeSosa asked.

"I told that nigga I didn't have nothing to do with the shit that happened to his brother. It was all Broady. He thought Phil killed his best friend, Razor, so he took revenge. I didn't have nothing to do with that," Junior explained. "But Phil hit my moms," Junior finished with venom. Nothing more needed to be said.

DeSosa seemed to contemplate what he was being told.

"Yes, I know everything, including the fact that you allowed a narco into my midst. Into my business!" DeSosa snapped, finally acknowledging Junior's confession.

"I didn't know Tuck was an undercover rat. It doesn't matter, anyway, does it? Aren't you untouchable?" Junior replied snidely. He was tired of the DeSosa bullshit.

DeSosa eyed him evilly. "You think Easy would've ever brought a rat into his company? You think he would've been that weak? You never were as good as he was at this business," DeSosa said cruelly, chuckling.

Junior swiped his hands down his thighs and shifted in his seat. He could feel heat rising in his chest. His eyes darted across the room at the two men standing around, trying to look casual, their weapons making visible bumps under their suit jackets. Junior knew better than to express his outrage. He was here to ask for help, after all.

"Do you remember the day Easy brought you to me, Junior?" DeSosa asked. The rolling *R* sent a cold chill down Junior's spine. "You were so poor, so pathetic. Coming from nothing," DeSosa said, curling his lip to show his disgust.

Junior swallowed hard. DeSosa liked to antagonize, and he knew just what to say to crush his opponent.

"You could never be Easy, eh, Junior, because you always make things so difficult for yourself." DeSosa laughed at his play on words.

Junior rolled his eyes to the ceiling. He couldn't escape Easy's shadow for the life of him. His lips formed a hard, straight line as DeSosa ripped into him.

"You were a skinny kid. Hungry to be a part of something. Easy was proud of the job he wanted you to do. He had given you the responsibility of taking the package . . . the same way he started out. Easy was always loyal when he trusted someone," DeSosa recounted, puffing on his cigar.

It was all too much: the words, the disrespectful smoke, the memories. Junior sat uncomfortably erect, uneasy. His hands were curled into fists; the veins in his wrists were bulging with restraint.

"Ah, yes, Easy Hardaway, the consummate humanitarian. He fed you. He taught you. He trusted you. *You* wanted to be *him*. I remember the day I met you. You stunk of envy. You reeked of animosity. I could see it in your eyes. You secretly hated the man who had fed and clothed you. From that day forward, I never trusted you. I knew when Easy wanted out, you would be the one I could count on to keep up the deal I had made with the devils, but I still didn't trust you. I knew you were so hungry for power that you would kill any man who stood in your way. You were born a snake. It is in your blood . . . a fucking cold-blooded killer like your father," DeSosa hissed cruelly.

Junior's temple throbbed and sweat beads lined up on his hairline like ready soldiers. His chest heaved at hearing the truth. If he hadn't been so outgunned, he would've slapped the shit out of the old man for speaking to him so disrespectfully. But DeSosa was no real threat to Junior. He was just an old bastard trying to assert himself like he was young and ruthless and in charge. Junior saw him for what he was: a shell of his younger self, a feeble old man racked by Multiple Sclerosis.

"Easy was not a saint. He killed one of my best friends, and he was a power hound. You know this. He only got out of the game because of Rock. A fuckin' hypocrite hit man acting as Easy's gotdamn moral compass," Junior denounced.

DeSosa stubbed his cigar out and dropped his hands at his sides. He pushed on the wheels of his wheelchair until his entire body emerged from around the table.

Junior looked at him without sympathy. He secretly wished he had been the one who'd put the bullet years ago into DeSosa that had taken away his ability to walk.

The "sniper's bullet" had been a hiccup in DeSosa's career, but it had not taken him out of the game. Now, though, the disease had done what a bullet couldn't do; it made him weak and vulnerable. Seeing his time on earth as limited, DeSosa was forced to tie up some loose ends from the past.

"Junior, I can help you with your problem with Phil, but I want you to find the girl. Easy's daughter. You know, the one who tried to kill you because she thought you killed Easy. I want her," DeSosa said, close enough for both the sweet and pungent smell of his cigar to lodge in the back of Junior's throat.

"I don't know where to find her," Junior replied in all honesty. He didn't want to make a two-sided deal. If he had to, he'd take care of Phil alone.

"Well, then, our business is done here," DeSosa said with finality.

Junior swallowed his pride. He knew he needed DeSosa, and he wanted to feel like DeSosa needed him.

"All right, man, tell me what you want me to do. But I want guarantees that I will be the fuckin' one to put a bullet in Phil's head. He hit my moms in her face," Junior growled.

"Good. Then we have a deal," DeSosa said ominously.

***

Avon drove to his home in Bowie, Maryland, for the first time since his meeting with the DEA and Grayson Stokes. He had to make sure his kids were safe. Stokes had scared the shit out of him. Now, as Avon pulled into the housing subdivision, he couldn't help but remember the last time he went home.

Avon had been undercover for almost an entire year and had not laid eyes on his family during this time. He had convinced himself that it was for their safety that he didn't call or visit while deep undercover. Instead, he received updates on his wife and kids from his case agent, Brad Brubaker.

When the line between "Avon, the agent" and "Tuck, the drug dealer" had become increasingly blurry, Avon decided it was time to go home for a reality check. For some time he'd felt the nagging urge to go home and hold his wife and kids. On that fateful day when he'd paid an unexpected visit home, he'd felt like a stranger.

Avon had sat outside and watched the house, mentally and emotionally preparing himself to reunite with a wife to whom he hadn't spoken in almost a year. He had desperately needed to get his mind right and shake the street persona he had assumed for the last year.

Unfortunately, Avon wasn't prepared to see Brad Brubaker walking out of his garage, or to watch his wife, Elaina, lovingly bestow Brubaker with the same smile she had given Avon so many times.

Avon reached for his gun when Brubaker kissed his wife on the lips and picked up Avon's daughter to kiss her on the forehead. They looked like one big happy family, and Avon felt like an outsider looking in. Avon racked the slide on his 9 mm Glock. He held it tightly in his sweaty hand as a small tornado of thoughts whipped through his mind. Avon closed his eyes and tried to squeeze back the tears as he watched his kids pile into Brubaker's car. Flexing his jaw in and out, Avon couldn't take it anymore. He mashed the gas pedal of the Lexus and it lurched out of hiding. Tires squealing, Avon drove a few paces and drove the car haphazardly onto the sidewalk in front of his house.

Elaina and Brubaker nearly jumped out of their skin.

Elaina's eyes stretched wide open. It looked as if her orbs would pop right out of their sockets.

Brubaker swallowed a hard lump of fear that had formed in the back of his throat. His face turned beet red, like a cooked lobster.

Avon leveled his gun at Brubaker's head.

"Avon, no!" Elaina screeched at the top of her lungs.

"Tucker . . . it's not what you think," Brubaker tried to explain; his hands were held high in surrender.

"I just saw you kiss my fucking wife!" Avon growled, his voice rising from the depths of his abdomen. Avon's hands were shaking and his lips were curled into a knot. He placed his gun against Brubaker's temple.

"Daddy! Stop it! Daddy!"

Avon heard his kids calling to him from the backseat of Brubaker's car. Avon's hands were shaking even more now; sweat dripped down his forehead.

The commotion brought neighbors from their homes. A few watched from their lawns; none dared to intervene in the family affair, particularly since firearms were involved. No doubt, a few had already called the police.

"Avon . . . please!" Elaina begged, tears cascading down her face. "I thought you were gone. He told me

*that you had left, turned on us. You never called," she
cried pitifully.*

*"So you fuck him? You don't wait to hear from me,"
Avon rebutted, his voice cracking. He kept his gun
firmly pressed to Brubaker's head.*

*"Daddy! Don't shoot him!" Avon heard his daughter
scream out again.*

*Her little voice had ultimately changed everyone's
fate that day.*

As Avon recalled the entire nightmarish scene, he
felt the same sharp tug in his heart. Avon blinked back
tears. All he could do now was hope that his kids had
forgiven him for making such a nasty scene. In the
meantime, he would focus all of his efforts on seeing
them to safety. He walked into his home to a hero's
welcome. It was as if the kids had forgotten about the
things that had happened. It had made Avon's heart
smile to get a neck hug from his little girl—a hug that
nearly choked him with its strength. Things with Elaina
were strained. Avon didn't let that deter his focus.

Once the pleasantries and hellos were over, Avon
wasted no time demanding that Elaina and the kids
pack up and go some place until he felt it was safe to
come home again. Although there were few places they
could go undetected, he felt fairly comfortable leaving
his wife and kids under the watchful eyes of Elaina's
parents.

So they headed there together.

Paranoid, Avon spent the first two nights at his in-
laws', staying there until he felt certain that his family
was in good hands. Avon sat up all night like a guard
dog, watching and waiting.

Avon hugged his kids and gave his mother-in-law a dry kiss on her cheek before leaving his family.

"Thanks for doing this, Helen. It won't be that long," Avon assured her.

Helen raised her eyebrows and crossed her arms over her chest; her displeasure was evident. Helen didn't appreciate the fact that his job had placed her daughter and grandchildren in jeopardy.

Although Avon and Elaina had tried to pretend that their visit was casual. Avon picked up his daughter and gave her a big kiss. She laid her head on his shoulders and asked him not to leave.

"I promise to come back soon. Mommy is going to be here with you, okay?" Avon assured. With his heart heavy, he placed his daughter back down on the floor and turned toward Elaina.

The tension that settled between them made him feel queasy. An awkward silence ensued. They hadn't said anything of substance to one another since he had returned and ordered them to pack their belongings in haste. After the first day, all of the pleasantries had dissipated between the two.

"How long are you going to be gone this time?" Elaina asked. Her voice was laced with resignation and irritation.

Elaina hugged herself in an attempt to quell the trembling that racked her body. She hung her head, unable to hold eye contact with her husband. He was a stranger to her now. His being gone so long without so much as a call or an occasional visit, then the affair—and now his frantic plea that she and the kids relocate—was simply taking its toll on her body and soul. Elaina felt Avon always put his need to succeed above all else in his life, including her and the children.

Avon let out a long, frustrated sigh. Though their relationship was strained, her safety was still important to him. And she had some nerve being angry with him, he silently groused.

"I don't know how long I'll be gone, but I want you and the kids to stay here until you hear from me." Avon needed to know that his wife and kids were out of harm's way.

Elaina shook her head from left to right and gnawed on her bottom lip. The pain and burden of it all was evident on both of their faces.

Elaina stepped closer to him, shifting her weight from one foot to the other. She reached out a trembling hand. "Look, Avon, for what it's worth . . . it didn't mean anything to me. It was the closest thing I had to you," Elaina confessed, her voice cracking and tears rimming her eyes.

He flinched and moved a safe distance from her grasp. Her words sent a sharp pang of hurt through Avon's chest. Elaina had been the first woman Avon truly loved. But she had also hurt him in the worst possible way. He knew his pride would never allow him to be with Elaina again, but divorce proceedings were the furthest thing from his mind right now.

Avon shoved his hands deep into his pockets to keep himself from reaching out and touching her. He wanted to embrace her, hold her face in his hands and tell her he was sorry for leaving and not calling. He wished he could explain that it had all been part of his job; it had all been for her safety. But he knew that wasn't entirely true, and they didn't need any more lies between them.

Her eyes begged him to understand, to love her again.

"I gotta go. I want you to stay inside the house as much as possible. Call me if you have to leave for longer than a few minutes," he finally said in an all-business tone.

Elaina had hoped to hear a glimmer of love or affection in his parting words. Instead, his parting words had been cold and formal. Without a glance backward, he turned his back on her and walked out of her life once again.

Avon pinched the bridge of his nose, hoping to release some of the tension in his head. He looked down at the box he had just hefted from his trunk. Digging inside, he pulled out the next notebook and began to lose himself in the story unfolding before his eyes. It was a necessary and welcome distraction.

He was starting to feel like he knew Easy. He could only imagine what a man who'd grown up like Easy must've gone through to protect his own family.

Avon Tucker was even more compelled to find Candy now.

Brooklyn, New York, 1986

"You see that bitch-ass right there?" Early asked.

Easy looked over and stared out the window on the side of the car Early sat on.

"You gon' jump out, blow that weasel's head off and get right back in here. You gotta earn ya wings. Ya dig?" Early said, still staring out the darkly tinted window.

Easy watched as the man walked out of the club with a woman on each arm. He wore a long, dark mink coat, a bloodred fedora and red alligator shoes. He chewed on the end of a toothpick in his mouth. The man's skin was the color of charcoal, and his eyes were beady like a snake's.

"He's a fake-ass pimp, ya dig. He owes me more than a little bit of bread, and I'm tired of waiting. He been in that club all night spreading my bread around like he Jesus feeding the hungry," Early told Easy.

"You just gon' kill him over some money?" Easy asked incredulously.

Early stared at the sixteen-year-old boy as if he were speaking a foreign language.

"Li'l nigga is you dumb, deaf or blind? Which one? I ain't gon' kill the muthafucka in the first place. You gon' kill this jive-ass weasel over my bread. And for the record, I'll kill a nigga just to prove a point, so what is you sayin'? I mean, if you scared, I can go find me a real soldier," Early demeaned. He didn't like to be questioned or second-guessed.

Easy had seen Early's wrath more than a few times in the three years he'd been living under the older man's tutelage.

"Um . . . no. I can do it. I—I ain't scared of n-nothing," Easy stammered. He didn't really have a choice.

Early had given him a home and a job since he had found him homeless and hungry. Early had offered him protection and introduced him to everybody who worked the streets. This task was simply part of the job. Easy owed him that much. If he refused the order, life as he knew it would be over.

"I thought you would come around," Early said, smirking. "Here. This baby will do the trick and ain't got a lot of recoil either. Nothing more reliable than this baby here." Early handed Easy a silver Colt revolver.

The gun felt as cold as ice in Easy's trembling bony hand.

"Now go on over there and return the favor I did for you when I got rid of your auntie's no-good husband."

Easy's heart hammered intensely; he felt like he was going to be bruised from the inside. Inhaling deeply, trying to calm his nerves, he grabbed the car door handle. His sweaty fingers slipped off the metal.

Early grabbed Easy's arm. "Calm down, li'l nigga. This is part of being a man on these streets," Early said.

Easy nodded his head up and down rapidly. He didn't even realize his eyes were blinking faster than a hummingbird's wings. Taking a deep breath, Easy finally got the car door open.

His target was bigger than he had appeared from the car. At six feet three inches tall, the man looked intimidating. The giant laughed; his voice was deep and guttural. Two women flanked him as they huddled together, sharing a white reefer joint.

Easy was walking fast now; his legs were seemingly moving on their own. His mind was adrift, blank. One of the women noticed Easy first.

"Aw, look at this little cutie-pie. You came to pay for some pussy, didn't you, baby bo—" Her words halted, and the smile plastered on her face crumbled into a look of abject horror.

Easy raised his hand and let off three shots into the man's face before the woman could shriek.

The man let out a scream that was nothing less than primordial. He staggered for a few seconds; his face seemed to break off and explode with each subsequent shot. His large body crumpled to the ground like a wall of bricks. The man's fedora lay under his head and served as a makeshift bucket for the blood leaking from his head.

Easy stood frozen with fear. His mind told him to run, but his body wouldn't cooperate. It was Early's booming baritone that finally spurned Easy into action.

"Get yo' ass over here!" Early barked.

Easy raced into the car. He was hyperventilating; his chest rose and fell so hard. He tried to swallow back the vomit. As the car sped down the streets, making hairpin turns, he lost all hope for keeping his cool. Easy placed his head between his legs and threw up the contents of his stomach.

"Damn, boy! I can tell this was your first time offing a nigga. Well, you can bet that it ain't gon' be your last. You gotta be that ruthless, nigga, on these here streets, baby boy. You gon' have to get used to this shit without losing your lunch."

Early laughed unsympathetically as Easy retched.

Chapter 6

The Insider

Candice pressed the doorbell and waited, tapping her left foot rapidly on the concrete step. She could feel sweat beads running a drag race down her back.

"Can I help you?" asked the woman who had snatched open the door.

Up close, her icy blue eyes and lemony blond hair had Candice stuck on stupid. Arellio DeSosa's wife looked as though she had just stepped out of the pages of *Vogue* magazine.

"Who are you and what do you want?" the beautiful Caucasian woman snapped, her forehead furrowed.

"I'm sorry. I am here from the agency . . . the nanny job." Candice stumbled over her words, her fake accent making her tongue feel foreign in her mouth.

She had been watching Flora long enough to know which agency she worked for and was finally able to get up the nerve to go inside and apply for the job.

The woman gave Candice the once-over and her face softened. At least they hadn't sent a beautiful young girl, like they usually did. Cyndi DeSosa wouldn't have to watch her husband around this little, fat, frumpy girl. There was an awkward pause as both women took measure of the other.

"Come in," the woman finally said, stepping aside from the door. "I hope you have your act together . . . not like that last one," Cyndi grumbled.

Candice felt slightly weak in the knees as she crossed the threshold of the DeSosa home. A funny feeling came over body; her nerve endings felt alive. She was inside! She was so close that she could hear the DeSosa woman breathing and smell her rich perfume.

Uncle Rock would've warned against this method. He liked to be the furtive hit man who took his targets by surprise. Candice was the opposite. She wanted to be near her victims, to witness their pain up close as she picked their lives apart, piece by piece.

"Did they tell you there were two children . . . little ones, very active," the woman explained.

Candice just nodded. Her brain was having trouble sending the right signals to her tongue. The room swayed around Candice and her ears rang. Her stomach had huge bat-sized butterflies bouncing around in it. The excitement and nervousness was overwhelming Candice.

"What's your name?" the woman asked as she noticed the glazed-over look in her eyes.

"Um . . . I—I am Dulce," Candice stammered, her horrible attempt at an accent coming and going like the uneven slopes of a mountain.

"Hmm, Dulce, like candy, is Spanish? Interesting," Cyndi commented.

Mrs. DeSosa wore slim-cut jeans, a pair of black patent leather stilettos and a close-fitting Lycra shirt that hugged her ample breasts. Simple but elegant—both at the same time. She had the body of a Victoria's Secret model.

"I'm Cyndi DeSosa . . . Mrs. DeSosa to you," the woman introduced rudely, not bothering to offer her hand. She needed to establish a strict employer-employee relationship early on. No more little bitches close to her kids, close to her husband.

"You have the papers from the agency?" Cyndi asked suspiciously.

Dumb ass. You should've asked before you let me in. I could've killed you and your family by now. Candice put on a fake smile and dug into her oversized purse, careful not to let the woman see her two best friends—Glock and SIG Sauer—lying snugly inside. Candice retrieved the paperwork and Cyndi snatched it from her hands. She looked at Candice and then back down to the paperwork.

"I only deal with people that Ms. Sanchez sends. Did she send you?" Cyndi looked at Candice with one raised, speculative eyebrow.

Candice thought about how she had put a gun to Flora's head, threatened her life and took all of Flora's agency paperwork. She'd then put the barrel of the same gun into Ms. Sanchez's mouth and told her that if she ever contacted the DeSosa family about her little visit, she would die. Both women had readily agreed, but Candice still left them with a nice gun butt scar to prove she meant business.

"Yes, she did. Ms. Sanchez sent me because Flora was fired for losing your son in the city or something like that," Candice relayed mendaciously.

Cyndi's facial expression grew dark; her eyes went into slits at the mere mention of Flora's name.

"That bitch is lucky to be alive," she said menacingly. "Let me show you around. I am very particular about my house, my children . . . and my husband," Cyndi said sternly, summoning Candice to follow her like a true subordinate.

Candice's knowledge of the incident had sealed the deal. She was officially in. She followed Cyndi through the beautiful house. It was clear that everything inside was expensive. It had all of the trappings of what Candice imagined a drug kingpin or a Mafia boss's house looked like. The inside boasted Italian marble floors, large gaudy accent pieces and shiny gold or black lacquer furniture. The vast window banks in the formal living room were dressed in gold and cream silk draperies, which looked as if they'd been imported from some faraway place. Gold and cream seemed to be the theme colors throughout. A bit opulent for Candice's taste, but definitely rich. Cyndi was obviously very proud as she pointed out her Picasso paintings and Kwan Yen statues. Candice tuned out Cyndi's boasts and took mental notes of doors, windows and things that could be obstacles to a fast break, if she ever needed to get out fast.

"Your sleeping quarters are upstairs, right next to the children," Cyndi continued.

As Candice followed Cyndi up the winding staircase, she looked intently at the gallery of family portraits on the long wall leading up the steps. She could probably name everyone in the pictures by now, and that made her smile inside.

When she got to the last step at the top, there it was: a larger-than-life portrait of their patriarch, symbolizing his position as head of the family. Candice's pulse quickened as she stared at the picture. He was older now; a jagged line of silver ran through his thinning dark hair. He was sitting in a wheelchair, flanked by his family.

Candice had read all about Rolando DeSosa getting shot. Behind them, a huge neon sign blazed in red letters: BAILE CALIENTE. Candice squinted her eyes into dashes. She couldn't peel her eyes away. *No emotions, Candy. No emotions right now.* Suddenly her right contact lens began to itch as her eyes started to well up with angry tears.

"That's my father-in-law. And that's my husband's and my club. He cut the ribbon that day," Cyndi explained after noticing her interest in the painting.

Candice nodded her head and smiled nervously. She wondered how long she'd been staring at the picture.

"You've seen him before?" Cyndi asked suspiciously, trying to see how much Candice knew about their family.

"Um . . . no. It's a nice picture, ma'am," Candice fabricated on the spot.

Cyndi gave her a sideways glance.

"Well, he used to be a very important and very dangerous man . . . not so much these days. He lives with us now and is winding down his life to be a grandfather and, finally, a father. I hope Ms. Sanchez told you the requirements of working here in this family. . . ." Cyndi looked at her expectantly.

Candice nodded.

They were both on the same page.

Mrs. DeSosa took Candice on a tour of the remainder of the 12,000-square-foot home.

"My father-in-law lives on that side of the house. He is a very sick man, and the kids only see him when he comes over here. He loves them, but they can sometimes be too much for a man in his condition," Cyndi explained as they passed through a long hallway leading to the off-limits wing of the house.

Candice knew she'd be venturing over there at some point. Cyndi told Candice she'd expect her to stay some nights because she often traveled with her husband or worked at the club late into the early-morning hours.

Candice met the children for the second time that week. The baby screamed as soon as Candice touched her soft, round cheeks, and little Rolando remained hidden behind his mother's legs. Candice wondered if the kids could tell that her hair, eyes, fat stomach and legs were all phony, just like her résumé. Children, in Candice's experience, were much more discerning about people's intentions than adults.

Cyndi didn't appear too concerned with her children's reluctance to meet their new nanny, however.

"They'll get used to you," Cyndi told her, only slightly embarrassed by her children's reactions.

Candice smiled and nodded in agreement. She'd have to get used to them too.

The most important thing for Candice was that she was within striking range of her targets, and close to bringing justice to her family.

Junior wrestled with the key in the old rusted door lock. His hands were sweaty and his heart was pumping hard and fast. He didn't know why he was so nervous to find out the truth, but he was. Junior told himself the only reason he had even come to Rock's apartment after all of this time was to get clues on Candy's whereabouts so he could turn her over to DeSosa like they'd agreed.

After Rock killed himself, Junior received the keys and a letter from Rock in the mail. Rock's punk ass had apologized for being an absentee father who had stood by and watched his son grow up rough. The note had informed him cryptically that there were things inside the apartment that would explain everything, but that he needed to be careful because enemies on both sides of the law would be watching him. Junior didn't give a fuck about any of that shit in Rock's final note. His sole purpose right now was hunting down Candy.

Junior entered the apartment and scrunched up his face in disgust. "How was this nigga living?" Junior whispered as he looked around at the shabby décor: old moth-eaten curtains, scratched and chipped wood furniture, mismatched table chairs, worn-out couch and holey chair.

He walked over to the coffee table; there was a box in the center. Junior peered inside and his heart leaped in his chest.

He had found what he was looking for.

After leaving the apartment, Junior rushed into Rolando DeSosa's office in a huff.

"I have an address for you," he blurted out. He wasn't going to tell DeSosa about the other things he'd found inside Rock's home.

"Very good, Junior. You work very fast," DeSosa commented.

"I really want this nigga Phil badly. He is hiding out, but I'm sure you have the power to find him," Junior cajoled.

DeSosa started laughing. "How about we take baby steps first. One man at a time," he said, extending his hand for the information Junior gripped to his chest.

Junior handed it over somewhat reluctantly.

"Go with them," DeSosa instructed, pointing toward his shadow men.

Without much of a choice, Junior did as he was told.

"Which one of y'all bitch niggas hit my moms?" Junior growled. His face was so close to Dray's that he could see the perspiration beads above the other man's clean lip.

"I don't know, man! I wasn't there!" Dray's arms burned as they were extended unnaturally far over his head. The metal chains dug into his wrists and his fingers had no feeling. They were already turning blue and purple from the lack of circulation.

One of DeSosa's goons walked in front of Dray's naked chest and laid his fist into Dray's sternum.

"Agh!" Dray screamed. His body bucked, which caused more pressure on the chains, and thus more pain.

"You still gon' act like you don't know shit about this? Phil is supposed to be your man, and you see what that shit got you?" Junior spat out. A large green vein was pulsing at his temple.

"Fuck you," Dray managed in a low growl, spitting up a mouthful of blood in Junior's direction. Dray wasn't going to let no Brooklyn cat make him into a pussy. If he was going to die, it was going to be on his feet and not on his knees.

"A'ight," Junior said, stepping back for a minute, swiping his hand roughly over his face. He nodded to the broad-shouldered Hispanic man whom DeSosa had assigned to assist him. The man rushed over and grabbed a gorilla fistful of Dray's balls.

"Agghh! Agghh!" Dray let out a bloodcurdling scream as the man exerted pressure on his man sac.

"You still don't wanna tell me who hit my moms, and where the fuck Phil is hiding?" Junior barked, extremely agitated. The area behind his eyes was throbbing.

Dray's head was hanging low; his chin was damn near touching the middle of his chest. He was too exhausted to scream anymore. Junior walked over to him, grabbed a handful of his hair and yanked his head upward.

"I said fuck you and your mom's nigga," Dray rasped.

Junior bit down on his bottom lip. He released Dray's head and pulled out his weapon.

"No, fuck you and your whole crew. They'll meet you in hell, bitch nigga!"

Junior leveled his gun at Dray's head and squeezed the trigger. He didn't stop shooting until the entire twelve-round magazine had been emptied into Dray's body.

"Get rid of him," Junior whispered harshly as he exited the room. "One down. One to go."

"In breaking news today, a mysterious shooting outside of Baile Caliente, a popular Latino salsa club, left two men dead. Police officials report that the shots seemed to have come from a distance, indicative of a sniper shooting," the newscaster said. "Police say that surveillance video in front of the club did not show any cars driving by or any shooters on foot. The two victims are rumored to work for Arellio DeSosa, the owner of the club and the son of the alleged former head of the Sindicato drug cartel. Arellio DeSosa's whereabouts at the time of the shootings were unknown. Police officials are combing the area looking for clues as to where the shots came from. We will continue to bring you live coverage as we receive updates."

Avon's head snapped up from the file he was reading when he heard the name "DeSosa" mentioned on the hotel television. "Shit!" he gasped, turning up the volume.

The shootings had Candy's signature written all over them. That was her modus operandi—take out her targets like falling dominoes. It was her way of building up to the big fish.

While working undercover for the past year, Avon had figured out that Candy was Easy's daughter and that she was out to avenge her family's deaths. When Candice had found out that Junior, Broady and Razor were not the ones responsible for the murders, but, in fact, it was her own brother, also named Junior, she had been devastated. Her brother had apparently been brainwashed by Rolando DeSosa to turn on his own father.

A lightbulb went off in Avon's mind. Candice was going after the most dangerous kingpin in the tristate area: Rolando DeSosa.

No wonder the fuckin' government was trying to find her—to keep her from assassinating their man.

Avon began pacing the floor. Candy was way out of her league. This was way different than fucking with a few street punks. She was playing a dangerous game now. Even more dangerous than the first time.

Avon had to contemplate his next move. He had been so immersed in the Easy Hardaway files that he'd lost sight of what he really needed to do . . . find Candy before the government or DeSosa did.

His cell phone rang, almost causing him to jump out of his own skin. Avon rushed over to the small desk in the far corner of the hotel room and looked at his phone. The number came up "unknown." It could be Elaina and the kids, he reasoned. He picked it up, with his nerves on edge.

"More people might die if you don't reconsider the deal I offered. That could've easily been Elaina or your son or your daughter. . . . Who knows who could go next?" Grayson Stokes threatened on the other end of the line.

Stokes's words coldly echoed in Avon's brain. He tightened his grip on the mobile device. His rushing breath was the only response Stokes received. His message had clearly hit home.

"Seems like our little friend is a trained assassin. I happen to know she's been trained by the best. I also happen to know where your family is, Agent Tucker," he rasped into the phone.

Avon closed his eyes. Why was he being put in the middle of this shit again? All he'd ever wanted was to be like his father—a good law enforcement officer who dedicated his life wholeheartedly to the job of bringing criminals to justice. Avon had made some mistakes along the way, yes, but nothing to warrant this sort of harassment.

"Let me find her on my own. I will bring her in," Avon finally spoke up. The only choice he had right now was to get down or lay down.

"Don't cross me, Agent Tucker. I don't like to be crossed. You should take example from Brad Brubaker. I hate liars and traitors," Stokes warned before hanging up the phone.

Avon looked at the phone for a long, hard minute. It had now become a matter of saving innocent lives. He snatched up the file he had been reading. He needed to know more.

Brooklyn, New York, 1988

Easy stood over Early's casket. He wanted to cry, scream, fight, spit and jump up and down—all at the same time. Early didn't look like himself. His face was extremely swollen and his lips looked like fish lips. The undertaker had told Easy that the shots Early had taken to his head made it hard for them to work with his natural face. They added a fair amount of wax and makeup for the open-casket service. Easy had protested against the casket being open, but he'd lost to Early's old lady, Syrita.

In fact, it was Syrita's ear-shattering screams that brought Easy out of his stupor in front of the casket. Syrita was making her way to the front of the funeral parlor in the most dramatic fashion possible.

Easy moved backward and took a seat in the front pew. He watched as one person after another came up to Early's casket to pay respects. Without a doubt, many of them simply wanted to assess the damage the bullet holes had done to his body.

Easy grew angrier by the minute. He was angry with himself for not being around when Early took the shots that sealed his fate.

Easy had been on his run, picking up an important package. The story went that Early was leaving the pool hall with Bosco, his right-hand man, when someone called his name real loud.

The street reporters said Early turned around; but before he could even blink, seven shots entered his head.

The story unsettled Easy, causing him severe stomach cramps. The method by which Early was murdered was nearly identical to the one he'd used two years earlier when he'd killed a man at Early's request. Easy felt in some degree responsible for Early's premature death, like it was Karma coming back to bite him in the ass.

Easy also felt more alone than he ever had in his life. So many street dudes hated Easy because of his association with Early. Now there was no one left to shelter or protect him. He must be his own man on the street. After the years he spent following Early like his shadow, he knew he could think, walk and talk like Early. And, most important, when need be, he could be as ruthless as Early as well.

Once Early was buried, Easy set out to make his mark. He had to stand on his own two feet now.

The first thing he did was move his belongings out of his makeshift room in the back of the pool hall. Easy got a room inside of an old rooming house in East

New York. He had a little money saved, so he decided to take a chance and go see the big man from whom he regularly picked up packages. Easy planned on convincing the man he could take over Early's operations on the street.

Easy stood in his spot on the corner, his hands shoved down into his pockets. It had been a year since he'd earned enough trust to get his own package. Though he was surrounded by loudmouthed wannabe gangsters, he never fed into their ways. He was always quiet and unassuming while conducting his hand-to-hand sales.

Easy had been out hustling all day and had almost finished his bundle when he was approached by a basehead named Charlotte.

"Easy, lemme get something on credit," Charlotte begged.

"Nah," Easy said in a low tone.

"C'mon . . . don't be like that. You usually hook a sista up," she pleaded.

"I said nah," Easy said firmly.

"You muthafucka! I'm one of your best customers and you just gon' put me off like that? You can't hook me up 'til check day?" Charlotte spat out, getting too close and too loud for Easy's comfort.

"Why don't you go ask one of them dudes," Easy said calmly, nodding toward his noisy counterparts. They were making fun of an older dude whom Easy had seen going into the store.

"You know your shit is the best out here. Stop playing!" Charlotte screeched. She nervously scratched against her arms.

"Yo, go 'head, man. I'm not giving you anything on credit." Easy dismissed her with a look of utter disgust.

Charlotte's skinny, poorly dressed frame made her look like she had one foot in the grave already. Her clothes hung off her bony body and she had visible dirt on her pants and the front of her shirt. Her hair was a wild bird's nest atop her head.

"Fuck you! You ain't shit, anyway. I know a couple of niggas who will beat ya ass and take all ya shit." Charlotte wagged a skeletal finger close to Easy's face. She hawked up a mucus-filled wad of spit and spewed it into Easy's face. Loud roars erupted from the rowdy corner boys. Easy had been played.

Easy quickly grabbed the bag-of-bones girl around her neck, lifting her off her feet. She dangled like a choked chicken. He scowled as he squeezed her neck without the least bit of conscience.

"Yo, kill that bitch!" one of the boys screamed out.

Easy was in a blind rage. He was about to catch a case.

"Yo, nigga, she about dead. That bitch turning purple!" someone yelled out.

It was the only thing that snapped Easy out of his rage; he couldn't commit murder in plain sight like this. He quickly came to his senses and dropped Charlotte back to her feet. She was coughing and rolling around wildly trying to catch her breath.

Easy lifted his foot and gave her a swift kick in the ass. "Don't let me see your fuckin' ass around here ever again!" Easy spat out.

Charlotte scrambled up off the ground, finally able to catch her breath enough to argue back.

"You gon' get yours, you bastard!" she rasped, still holding her bruised neck.

"*Get the fuck outta here, you dirty bitch!*" *Easy called after her.*

A man exited the bodega behind him, and the next thing Easy knew he felt a rush of wind and a pair of hands pushing him out of the way. The old black dude from the bodega was taking down a man in a black leather trench coat who held a gun in his hand. Easy's heart began to pound as he watched the older gentleman clamp down on the gunman's wrist. The gunman cried out in pain and the gun skittered to the ground.

When the guys on the corner noticed the commotion, they all began to scatter. "*Oh shit, a gun!*" *they yelled. The last thing they needed was for the cops to come around.*

Easy couldn't move; he was in shock.

The stranger calmly picked up the gun, dropped the magazine out of it, dismantled the slide and threw the bottom half of it at the guy on the ground.

"*Oh shit! That bitch tried to set me up!*" *Easy finally found his voice, his heart racing as he realized what had just happened.*

The old dude nodded in agreement.

"*Fuck! Thank God you were here. That nigga woulda shot me right in the back of my fuckin' head,*" *Easy concluded.*

The old dude nodded again, but still did not speak a word.

"*I'ma fuckin' kill him!*" *Easy screamed, his blood boiling.*

The old dude put his hand up to Easy's chest to stop him.

"*Not here. Not now.*" *The old dude finally spoke.*

Easy backed down. Something about the stranger's calm, fatherly words struck him as soothing. In some ways the man reminded him a lot of Early.

"I'm Eric. But everybody calls me Easy," he said, introducing himself.

"Rock," the old dude said, taking Easy's extended hand and shaking it firmly.

"Yo, man, how can I repay you for that shit?" Easy asked earnestly.

"No need," Rock said, handing Easy the magazine full of .40-caliber rounds and the slide of his would-be assassin's gun.

"Nah, there has got to be something. Some money, some food, clothes, something," Easy offered. He didn't like feeling indebted to any man.

"Just go inside and get my BC Powder. I have the worst headache," Rock said calmly.

Easy scrambled to do as Rock had asked.

What had started out as a chance encounter quickly blossomed into a friendship.

Easy and Rock had only been friends for four months when Easy went to Rock for advice about an offer he thought he couldn't refuse.

"This dude Rolando DeSosa is the man up in Spanish Harlem. He came looking for me the other day," Easy told Rock.

Rock rubbed his chin, digesting the information. "If he is 'the man,' like you say, why would he come looking for a corner boy like you?" Rock asked logically.

"Because he heard I was 'the man' out here in Brooklyn. I guess Chulo, the dude I was getting my package from, told him about me. How I'm moving my shit like no other cat out here," Easy boasted with excitement.

"It just doesn't sound right. Be careful," Rock said ominously.

"Nah, man, this is my come up. Besides, I got you to protect me, right?" Easy laughed.

Rock nodded in all seriousness. He had heard the name DeSosa before, but he couldn't for the life of him remember in what context. He'd definitely be keeping a close eye on young Easy in the meantime.

Chapter 7

Learning Lessons

Candice grips the down pillow tightly in her hands. Her forehead drips with sweat. She stands ominously over the sleeping form, watching the sheet move gently with each slow breath. Candice's chest rises and falls rapidly—part excitement, part fear.

She will have to be strong enough to withstand the fight. The bucking and thrashing will probably be severe at first. The human body can become quite powerful when fighting to stay alive; this was one of Uncle Rock's many lessons.

She has been waiting a long time for this. Her arms jerk involuntarily toward her victim. Candice closes her eyes and lowers the pillow over the nose and mouth. She applies the pressure of her entire body weight on top of the pillow. She feels the figure come alive.

A short, muffled scream splits the air; then frantic, louder screams ensue.

Candice pushes down harder. Her victim's hands valiantly fight, grasping at the pillow material in an attempt to propel the assailant off his body.

Candice exerts all of her body weight over the thrashing form. The head attempts to turn sideways, but Candice bunches her forearms and strengthens her hold. The muscles in her arm cord against her skin.

The thrashing is worse than she'd anticipated. The torso bucks just before the screams fade against the material. Candice is being scratched and slapped by the hands now.

She takes it.

She gnashes her teeth and wills the force of gravity to aid her in her endeavor. The abuse Candice endures is short-lived. She feels the arms go weak and drop down to the side of the limp body.

One last body jerk and it is all over.

Candice stands proudly above the victim, congratulating herself on a job well done. She picks up the pillow to take a look at her handiwork. She wants to see the lifeless face and feel the satisfaction of knowing she can at last be at peace.

Candice's heart comes to a stop.

Her father's face gazes back at her with wide, vacant eyes.

"No!" Candice woke up, screaming out loud. Her nightgown clung to her chest, soaked in sweat. Candice blinked her eyes rapidly, trying to collect her thoughts. A round of loud knocks on her door forced her to get her bearings quickly.

"Dulce! Are you awake?" Cyndi called out from the other side of the door.

Candice looked around the room. *Shit!* She jumped up and wrapped a thick robe around her fat suit.

"Dulce!" Cyndi impatiently called out again.

Candice quickly padded over to the door and pulled it back. A fine sheen of sweat still covered her head.

Cyndi looked at her suspiciously.

Candice was immediately concerned that her wig was twisted or maybe her fat suit was hanging the wrong way.

"Are you all right?" Cyndi asked.

Candice hugged herself, still visibly shaken from her too vivid dream.

"I'm fine. Just stayed up late with the baby—that's all," she said, almost forgetting to add her accent.

Cyndi eyed her up and down. She didn't have time to deal with Dulce's odd behavior right now.

"We are heading to the funerals. Everyone is going, so it'll just be you and the kids today," Cyndi said solemnly.

Just a week ago Cyndi had been crying and upset when she'd come home from work.

"What's the matter, Mrs. DeSosa?" Candice had asked innocently, her forehead furrowed for good measure. Of course, she had already heard the story on the news, but she wasn't about to let on to her employer that she had been following the story so closely.

Cyndi took one look at Dulce, her nanny, and collapsed onto her chest with racking sobs.

Candice didn't know what to do. So she stood stockstill, hoping that Cyndi would be so caught up in her grief that she wouldn't feel the fakeness of her ample stomach and breasts, or smell the caked-on makeup coating her face, or notice her contact lenses.

Candice pried Cyndi's arms from her body and moved her to the cream leather sofa, which was rarely sat upon. In the end Cyndi had just wanted someone who would listen to her and feel her pain.

"There was a shooting at Baile Caliente," Cyndi sobbed, swiping at her eyes with an overused, crushed tissue.

"Oh no," Candice commiserated, giving her Academy Award–worthy performance.

"Yes . . . and my brother . . . my brother . . ." Cyndi was crying, barely able to get the words out.

"Did something happen to your brother, Mrs. DeSosa?" Candice asked softly, trying very hard to keep her excitement at bay.

"He is dead! They killed him!" Cyndi wailed.

Her words had sent a surge of satisfaction over Candice's body that felt better than an orgasm. She sat silent and relaxed as Cyndi DeSosa continued to pour her heart out to the hired help.

"I hope you'll be okay today," Candice said, snapping out of her reverie. She was sure to lay the accent on thick this time.

"I don't know how I'm going to stand watching my mother mourn for her only son," Cyndi replied, tears welling up in her eyes.

Candice looked at the pain in her eyes and actually felt some sympathy for the woman. She wondered if Uncle Rock had seen that same pain in her own eyes when she'd lost her family.

"I understand your pain. I lost two brothers myself," Candice said without thinking. It was a slipup, but she didn't regret the words at all. She was witnessing a pain she had already experienced.

Cyndi seemed slightly caught off guard by Candice's admission, but her face quickly softened. "Oh, Dulce, I'm very sorry. I can only imagine what you must've gone through. I never want to think about anyone experiencing the pain that I feel right now," Cyndi lamented.

Candice looked at her and tried hard to feign sympathy.

"Cyndi, let's go!" a man's voice boomed from the bottom of the stairs.

Candice and Cyndi both jumped, but for different reasons.

Cyndi closed her eyes tightly and exhaled a windstorm of exasperated breath.

"Dulce, I have to go. Please kiss the kids for me when they wake," Cyndi said softly. She cracked a small smile, satisfied that she'd chosen the right nanny this time around. Cyndi turned to walk away and Candice followed her with her eyes.

When she'd disappeared down the steps, Candice walked to the edge of the staircase balcony, watching the DeSosa family. They were like one solid unit, comforting each other. Arellio placed his hand on the small of Cyndi's back, ushering her forward, while his brother, Guillermo, navigated his father's wheelchair.

It was the first time Candice had seen all three men gathered together. Heat rose from her feet and settled in her chest. She gripped the railing to keep herself from screaming out. Watching DeSosa with his sons reminded Candice of her own father and brothers.

Hardaway Household, 2005

Errol and Eric Jr. were Easy's two eldest children. They were twins, but polar opposites. Even as little kids, Errol was always quiet and reserved; he was the one who thought all of his actions through before making a move. Eric Jr., whom everyone called Junior, had always been the one to act first and think later.

Easy had a close relationship with both of his sons. As soon as they were potty trained, Eric had the boys play every Little League sport imaginable—soccer, basketball, baseball, football—you name it; they played it. He also did typical father-son activities like watching professional sports together and going camping with their Boy Scout troops.

As the boys got older, though, things started to change.

"Get the fuck off me! I hate you!" Eric Jr. screamed as he fought against Easy's death grip.

"Calm the fuck down, boy! What has gotten into you?" Easy tried to restrain his son, using his arms as a human straitjacket.

Eric Jr. gnashed his teeth and thrashed his body wildly, bucking like a wild animal. It was like some unknown force had taken over him.

Easy was seriously struggling to maintain his grip. The gangly sixteen-year-old was almost as big as his father now. It wasn't as simple anymore as holding him down until the fight left his body. Easy's arms were aching and his back stinging. His son seemed to gain strength by the minute.

"I'ma kill you! I'ma kill you!" Eric Junior threatened now; his lip was bleeding from his own teeth biting down into it.

The entire house was awake now.

"Oh my God! What is going on?" Corine cried out as she raced to the scene. She had been worried about her son lately. His violent outbursts had become more and more frequent. It was like she didn't even know her own child.

"I said, get the fuck off me! I'ma fuckin' blow your brains out!" Junior screeched.

Easy was so shocked that he loosened his grip for just a minute. His son broke free, like a caged animal turned loose. He turned on his father and stood toe-to-toe with him. Junior's eyes were wild; mucus ran out of his nose, sweat covered his face, and his chest was swollen like someone had inserted a balloon under his shirt.

"They told me to kill you! You are the enemy!" Eric Junior hissed. The fire was visible in his eyes.

Lately Junior's behavior had become increasingly erratic; he continued to threaten his father with bodily harm and violence. His behavior was characteristic of a schizophrenic.

Easy sighed with deep regret and sadness. The "voices" were obviously telling him to kill his father.

"You better sit the fuck down," Easy barked. Sometimes the easiest way to handle his son was to take a no-nonsense approach. He took a few steps away from his crazed son in the event that Junior decided to strike him.

"Eric Junior, please! Stop it!" Corine screamed now. Junior looked at his mother for a minute with a fiery glare. The look in his eyes chilled Corine to the bone.

"What is the matter, baby?" she whined. Her head was tilted in dismay and confusion. Corine had never come to terms with the fact that her oldest son had serious psychological issues. "Please, baby, just listen to your daddy" she pleaded, trying to reach the innocent baby boy she knew lurked inside. Her words appeared to fall on deaf ears.

Eric Jr. growled like a lion in heat and charged into his father like a wrecking ball crashing into an old landmark. The demons inside him had full control of his limbs.

"Oh my God! No!" Corine screeched as her husband went crashing to the floor. The back of his head slammed into the hardwood floor. He lay still for a few seconds; Corine feared that Easy had been knocked unconscious.

Junior was on top of his father immediately after the fall, pummeling his dad's face and head with punches.

"They told me to kill you!" Eric Jr. growled again. "I have to kill you!"

"Who are you talking about? Who told you to kill your father?" Corine cried out. She hoped her son wasn't hearing voices in his head again. They had taken him to several psychiatrists. However, each time they wanted to put him on medication, Corine had refused. She was regretting her decision now.

The entire house was awake now; the commotion had roused them all from their sleep.

Candice rushed down the steps toward the noise.

"Daddy!" she screamed, her mouth and eyes wide at the sight.

Easy groggily regained his bearings. He put his hands up in defense and grabbed his son around the neck. Easy picked his throbbing head up off the floor slightly and applied pressure to his son's neck. He squeezed and squeezed and squeezed. Junior's body began to go limp; saliva dribbled from his lips and his face turned a garish shade of purple.

"Eric, you're gonna kill him! Stop it!" Corine screeched at an ear-shattering pitch.

Errol nearly barreled over the heap of tangled body parts. This was not the first time he pried his father loose from his brother's deranged grip. This time, however, it was his brother's neck that needed to be rescued from his father's brutal clutch.

"Daddy!" Candice screamed, jumping up and down. She was crying hysterically.

It was her voice that snapped Easy out of his murderous trance. Easy's grip relaxed; Errol managed to pull his brother's limp body away from his father.

Easy stood up; the room swayed around him. He looked at his son, who lay on the ground, coughing and rolling around, gasping for air. Easy had come so close to taking his own son's life. He couldn't understand what was going on with the kid.

"Are you all right, baby?" Corine bent down at her son's side. "What's the matter with him? It's like he's on something!" she cried out, looking to Easy for some explanation.

Easy couldn't call it. His son's behavior had grown more and more erratic lately. Easy had never put two and two together that his son's behavior had gone off the chart right around the time Easy had started grooming his boys to join the family business. He was too preoccupied with his feelings of failure that one of them was clearly mentally unstable. He'd lost a lot of sleep over the matter lately. He was beginning to think that Junior needed medication to keep his moods in check.

"Daddy" Candice whispered as her father stormed out of the room, disappearing in his office. Candice approached the closed door and debated whether or not to knock before she entered. She could hear her father talking on the phone.

"Rock! I need to see you right away. This shit is a matter of life and death," Easy had rasped into the phone.

Why did her brother and father have to fight all of the time? And what was her father planning with Uncle Rock? Candice slid down the wall, onto the floor, and began sobbing. She just wished her family could all get along with each other. She felt totally helpless, caught between a deep love for her father and sympathetic feelings for her brother, whom she'd watch spiraling out of control.

***

Candice crept around Rolando DeSosa's living space. It smelled of liniment and hospital disinfectant—not exactly a smell she would expect to find in the lodgings of a self-proclaimed "Scarface" type of kingpin.

Candice felt anxious as she walked through the man's private rooms. She glanced at the bed and wished she could just place a poisonous snake under DeSosa's covers and be done with it. But she had some digging to do first. She quickly headed to the small makeshift office. A cherry wood desk with pictures of his sons and grandkids sat atop the desk. The bookshelves were also sprinkled with family photos, much like Candice's father's own office. She rifled through the drawers of the desk, looking for any important documents. What she came across was mostly hospital bills, utility bills and random notes. Frustrated, Candice tossed the papers back into the drawer.

In the long drawer in the center of the desk, where one usually stored pens, pencils and other small desk essentials, she found a single photograph. Candice felt a chill come over her, like someone had pumped ice water into her veins. She swallowed the golf ball–sized lump of fear at the back of her throat and willed herself to calm down. Reaching out tentatively, she picked up the photograph. She clapped her hand over her mouth to keep herself from screaming at the image of herself. DeSosa had some handwritten notes on the top: *Easy Hardaway's living daughter. Find and turn over to Stokes for reward.*

Candice gripped her chest, trying to keep her heart from beating too fast. Uncle Rock had told her the government would be looking for her, but she didn't realize how close she was to being found. Candice dropped the picture back into the drawer. She decided it was time for her to step up her game; it was do or die for her. She rushed blindly out of DeSosa's living quarters and headed back to her room.

A lone figure stood at the end of the hall and watched the new nanny furtively exit DeSosa's private quarters.

"Tucker, you can't just assume that these people are bluffing," Dana Carlisle said as she watched Tuck pace the floor of her apartment for the fifteenth time.

"They're not going to fuck with my family," he huffed, hoping that his speaking the words would make them somehow true. The truth was he didn't know what to expect from Grayson Stokes or the DEA for that matter. They were all corrupt in his eyes.

"Well, now she's out there killing off their people. Getting closer and closer to DeSosa," Carlisle recounted.

He had told Carlisle all about his call with Grayson Stokes after the Baile Caliente shootings. Everyone just assumed it was Candy; that had been Tucker's first assumption as well. But now he was plagued with doubt. He had come back to Carlisle's house because he needed help reading through the Hardaway books. If they worked together, the puzzle pieces would start falling into place a lot faster, and they could finally see the big picture. At this point Carlisle was his best and only option.

"You really think it's her? I'm not sure I believe that anymore," Tuck countered. He knew Candy. He had spent almost two months with her. Though she was trained well, he didn't think she was capable of cold-blooded murder.

"That's exactly what she wants you to think . . . that she isn't capable of killing. She wants everyone to think that. But the government ain't buying it," Carlisle said pointedly.

Tucker roughly wiped his hands over his face and let out a deep breath. He walked over to the piles of books scattered on the floor and dining table.

"I guess we better keep reading for now. We don't have that much time, and I need to be armed with the truth this time," he said in a resigned voice. He lifted the cover of the next set of books and flopped down on the couch. Dana Carlisle perched herself on the back of the couch and began reading over his shoulder.

"Yeah, I'm hoping somewhere beneath all of this conspiracy theory bullshit is the truth," she said, scanning the paper for relevant information.

Brooklyn, New York, 2006

Easy and Rock sat across from each other, gauging the other's thoughts.

"I don't know if I can do what you're asking me to do, Rock," Easy said, breaking the tense silence that had settled in the room.

It wasn't what Rock wanted to hear.

Rock closed his eyes and tilted his head to the side. Easy's words stung like a swarm of angry yellow jackets. Already a man of few words, this topic left his stomach reeling. He planned his words very carefully, not letting on too much. It had been a hard decision to ask Easy to leave the game. Especially now, when Easy was at the top, riding high.

Easy had graduated from pushing packs of heroin to running the entire crack cocaine game in Brooklyn. That was what made Rock so sick to his gut.

Rock cleared his throat roughly; the grating sound causing Easy to jump a bit. The tension in the room was palpable now. Easy had always taken Rock's advice; in turn, Rock had served as Easy's loyal "cleaner." But perhaps he was asking too much of Easy.

"I can't tell you what to do. I can only advise you to get out of the game now. I've heard that DeSosa is working with some very dangerous people," Rock said, his tone ominous.

"How do you know anything about DeSosa? I know you never liked him, but you've never told me why," Easy said, frustration mounting in his voice. He respected Rock, but right now Rock was overstepping his boundaries.

Rock looked at Easy, square in the face. "I know more than you think."

"Here you go with the conspiracy shit, Rock. C'mon, man, all that crap is TV bullshit. I've listened to your stories, but I'm not about to make an important life decision based on your crazy-ass thoughts." Easy was trying to keep his composure now.

Rock was quiet. He looked different, like he had been up all night in a fight and had barely come out of it alive.

Easy eyed him closely. He appreciated everything Rock had done for him over the years. He didn't want a beef with his old mentor.

"I have been in the game almost twenty years now, Rock. I moved up. I'm finally at the top. You have to understand that," Easy said, softening his tone while trying to level with Rock. "I can't say no to DeSosa just cuz you telling me I should quit because you got a bad feeling about my connect." He needed Rock to understand where he was coming from.

"Look here!" Rock barked, coming alive. He fisted his hands on his knees and shifted his jaw. Rock closed

his eyes and tried to use a meditation technique to keep himself from jumping out of his chair. He looked crazier than Easy had ever imagined.

"What's up with you, man?" Easy asked, alarmed at his friend's angry demeanor.

Rock took a deep breath. "Easy, this is something you have to do. Don't ask any more questions. Call up DeSosa and tell him you're leaving the game. You have to trust me on this," Rock said, his voice full of concern.

Rock stood up. His large body cast a dark shadow over Easy. Easy gazed up at Rock. He had trusted this man with his life—literally—from day one.

"I'll think about it," Easy said, trying to hide his frustration.

"You better not think about it too long," Rock warned before rushing out of the room.

Easy contemplated the consequences of actually carrying out Rock's order, but he needed to discuss a few things with DeSosa first. Easy dialed DeSosa's number, but he quickly hung up when it started to ring.

He needed to think this out a bit. Telling DeSosa he was leaving the game would be no easy task. He needed to talk to Rock first and figure out a plan for disengaging himself. Extricating himself from DeSosa's network certainly would not be as simple as a phone call.

Chapter 8

Dangerous Encounters

Junior pulled up to the DeSosa home, like he'd done every three days for the past several weeks. He rushed inside and was frisked at the door—the normal routine. Junior was nervous for some reason; he had a strong premonition that today wasn't going to be a good day.

DeSosa was sitting with his back turned toward the door, but he felt Junior's presence. A long, awkward silence ensued.

Junior opened his mouth to fill the choking silence, but he wasn't able to get a word out.

"So what do you have for me?" DeSosa asked without turning around. Cigar smoke danced around his head and colored the air a hazy gray.

Junior cleared his throat. He had been dreading this meeting, since he had nothing substantive to report. He balled up his toes in his shoes, rocking on the balls of his feet.

"DeSosa, man . . . I'm—I'm . . . sorry," Junior stammered. He cleared his throat again. He wondered if DeSosa, like Junior's mother, would be able to tell he was lying just from the shaking in his voice. "No new updates. I been to the apartment she used to stay in and it was trashed, but she wasn't there. I don't know where else to look . . . I mean. . . ," Junior continued, glad to have gotten his lie out without pause.

He had no intention of trying to find Candy; and if he did, it wouldn't be to turn her over to DeSosa. Junior needed DeSosa's help getting at Phil. His crew had fragmented after everything went down with his brother, so he'd never be able to face up to Phil and his boys. Now that Dray was dead, Junior knew Phil would be after his head; and maybe this time he'd even come after Junior's own mother.

"For some reason, Junior, I don't believe you," DeSosa snapped. His face was drawn into a scowl; the look sent chills down Junior's spine.

"Well, I'm telling you the truth. I have no idea where she is or where to find her," Junior said, false frustration lacing his words. He had to make it look and sound believable. His sheer frustration with trying to find Candy, the gotdamn assassin, had consumed his days and nights.

"Well, then, Junior, our business is finished. We have no more to discuss until you bring me what I want. I can't give you Phil without assurance that I will get what I want. Looks like our deal is off. You can go," DeSosa rasped dismissively.

Junior felt like a kid who'd just been suspended from school. He looked around the room, then back at DeSosa. He knew DeSosa too well; it would never be over that easily.

"C'mon, DeSosa! I'm sayin', how the fuck do you expect me to find this bitch? I don't know where she is! I hardly even know her! I find out this punk-ass old man who raised her is my own fuckin' father, but that don't mean I know where to find this bitch! I told you everything. . . . I gave you every fuckin' thing I could!" Junior forcefully detailed. He was on the brink of tears. "You, of all people, should understand why I want Phil! If somebody did something to your family, you would be the first one out for blood!" Junior whined now, pleading his case.

DeSosa's henchmen closed in on him, but he didn't care. He was coming apart right now. His business had dried up. DeSosa was no longer supplying him because he thought he might still be a target of the DEA. And now he'd never be able to get his hands on Phil.

"DeSosa! You can't do this to me now!" Junior pleaded.

DeSosa didn't flinch or blink. He didn't have any respect for a man who couldn't stand his ground. That was the one thing that had set Easy apart in DeSosa's mind. Although he ultimately viewed Easy as a traitor, which was the most detestable form of human being, at least he could respect Easy for sticking to his decision about turning his back on the game.

"You can leave now. When you find out any information, you are welcome to come back. Maybe by then you'll grow some balls and find some loyalty," DeSosa spat out in Junior's direction. His words cut like small carving knives.

"Fuck you, DeSosa! Fuck you and your little game!" Junior boomed. His newfound courage wrapped around him like a dark cloak.

DeSosa let out a snort, followed by a maniacal laugh. His goons surrounded Junior now. Junior wrestled his arm away from the big gorilla-shaped goon who roughly helped him to the door.

He straightened out his rumpled jacket sleeve and followed their lead to the door. Before he got there, he stopped in his tracks to address DeSosa. His action garnered glares from the goons.

"You really fucked up for this one. You just gonna leave me out there like that after I mirked Phil's right-hand man at your request? Those niggas are looking for me and you just gonna leave me open out there with no help and no protection? I'm tellin' you, what goes around comes around. . . . You better sleep with one eye open." Junior issued his warning; his voice was quaking—filled with one part anger, one part fear.

His words got him grabbed by the neck by a goon.

"You are weak! You can't find one girl who tried to fuckin' kill you! I have nothing to say to you! Get the fuck out of my presence!" DeSosa barked at Junior's back.

Junior was tossed outside the house like yesterday's trash. His ego was bruised, and so were both of his knees.

"I want him followed. I think he knows something and he is just not letting on." DeSosa snapped his orders, flicking his hand in the direction of the door. He needed some time to regroup and rethink this whole situation with the girl.

Outside, Junior picked himself up off the concrete ground and shouted for DeSosa and the world to hear. "Y'all ain't seen the last of me! You muthafuckas fucked with the wrong nigga!"

He stepped backward out of the gate, when he spotted a woman out of the corner of his eye. She was herding two little kids in the opposite direction of the commotion. He was angry, but for some reason he took particular notice of her. Maybe it was because she watched the scene a bit too closely.

"Mind yo' fuckin' business, bitch!" Junior yelled at the unsuspecting nanny.

The woman scampered into the house with the children in tow like he was a pedophile on the sex offender registry. Something about the fat, frumpy nanny made Junior pissed. She had the nerve to be watching *him* get embarrassed.

Junior waited outside the gate for DeSosa's thugs to bring his car around. He needed to get far away from this place and come up with a new strategy for finding Phil and catching that cunt, Candy.

Tuck slumped down farther into his seat as he watched Junior get tossed out of DeSosa's estate. Then Tuck noticed the woman who watched from the sidelines, much like himself. Something inside his chest jumped; her face was disguised but familiar.

"Candy," he whispered, his breath catching. Tuck forgot everything: the danger, his cover, her cover, everything. He was up in his seat now, with his dark glasses far down on his nose. He needed to see her in natural light. He needed to know if it was really Candy or if his mind had conjured up her image.

Candice glanced in his direction as she hefted a baby girl onto her hip and grabbed the little boy's hand. Tuck watched her rush away—her body not the same, but her eyes telling a different story.

Tuck was brought back to reality when Junior revved his car engine. With his heart sitting in the back of his throat, Tuck shrank back down into his seat. He would sit outside all night if he had to until Candy emerged.

Tuck's mind was too preoccupied to realize that he was being followed as well.

One of DeSosa's henchmen picked up his cell phone to call in his report. "*Sí*, tell the boss he was right. Junior is being followed by the DEA agent. I have my eye on him right now. He is watching the house." The man relayed his visuals into the phone.

He could hear DeSosa's booming voice in the background. He cursed Junior's name and condemned him to hell for being a traitor. The man listened, knowing that Junior had sealed his fate.

The one thing DeSosa couldn't stand was a traitor. He viewed them as low-down, dirty scum of the earth. It was the same reason Easy Hardaway had suffered the fate that he did. DeSosa finished his tirade with specific instructions.

Neither Junior, Tuck nor Candy was safe.

Candice rushed the children back into the house. Her head was spinning. She'd seen Tuck and she knew that he'd seen her.

What the fuck is he doing there? How did he find me?

He'd definitely recognized her; she was sure of it. She didn't want to believe Tuck was part of the government bastards who were after her. But now he appeared to be spying on her, and she had to reconsider. Could it be that he was just another hired gun after her head?

Candice felt sick to her stomach. His betrayal burned badly. Candice's hand shook and her body was covered with a fine sheen of sweat. The fat suit felt extremely heavy on her body and her legs felt wobbly. Stumbling around like a cow, she could barely carry the baby up the stairs. Candice reached to the wall for support and caused one of the pictures to crash to the floor. Candice jumped, her nerves on edge. She looked down at the shattered glass frame that held a picture of Guillermo. Candice stared at the picture like it was a bad omen. She felt like throwing up.

Cyndi rounded the corner like a bat out of hell in response to the loud noise.

"Dulce, are you all right?" she asked, noticing Candice's pained expression. Cyndi looked down at the shattered frame, then back up at Candice.

"Um . . . I—I'm not feeling good. I need to leave early, if you don't m-mind," Candice stammered, using the wall to hold herself up now. She couldn't even be bothered with the accent, and she didn't even care if Cyndi noticed.

Cyndi eyed her suspiciously and grabbed her baby before Dulce dropped her.

"I have to go," Candice panted; her chest felt tight. She was afraid that if she stood in front of Cyndi another minute, she would definitely blow her disguise.

Candice slid down the steps and out of Cyndi's line of vision.

"Okay. Okay, you go ahead. I'll keep the kids tonight," Cyndi called out from the balcony landing.

All Candice wanted to do was get out of the house and take in a deep gulp of fresh air. She moved fast now, ignoring everyone and everything.

As Candice moved away from her, Cyndi noticed that her nanny's shirt was hiked up slightly in the back. Cyndi squinted; Dulce's skin looked wrinkled and rubbery. Perhaps she had been burned in a fire as a child? Cyndi shook her head. Maybe her eyes were deceiving her, or the lighting was bad, but a nagging, suspicious feeling invaded her mind.

Something about Dulce just didn't sit right with her, and she couldn't put her finger on it. She had a funny feeling about her from day one, but she'd ignored it. With everything that had happened, she had been preoccupied, but the feeling was back. Cyndi hurried up the stairs and put her baby down in the crib. She rushed to her bedroom and retrieved her cell phone.

"Hello, Ms. Sanchez? I need to ask you some questions about the nanny you sent to replace Flora. Yes, I want to know everything," Cyndi demanded.

***

Tuck watched the chubby Hispanic woman rush through the gates of the DeSosa home. He started up his engine as soon as she got in her car; in a matter of seconds he was on her tail.

"You are a bold bitch, Candy," he said out loud to himself. He could not believe she was inside DeSosa's home, playing with his grandkids. He thought Candy had been bold when she infiltrated Junior's crew to get closer to them, but this took the cake. She was one bad bitch, and he knew he'd have to tread lightly with her.

He followed Candice with every dip, turn and U-turn she made. He had to give it to her—she was slippery as a snake. Rock Barton had obviously trained her well.

Candice pulled her car over abruptly. Tuck had to stop short to keep from rear-ending her.

"Fuck!" Tuck cursed, slamming his palms on the steering wheel. He had been made.

Candy rushed toward his car, digging into her bag at the same time. Tuck went to his waistband as well. She yanked open his passenger door and plopped into the seat. Her gun was under his chin, and his was at her temple.

"Why the fuck are you following me?" Candice growled. Her finger was in the trigger guard, ready to blow Tuck's head off.

"I'm not following you! I was following Junior!" Tuck panted, his nerves on a hair trigger.

"You're a fucking liar! How did you know it was me?"

"I recognized you, even with all of that padding, makeup and fake-ass eyes! What made you think you could disguise your eyes?" Tuck's voice cracked. He still seemed to have a soft spot for her.

"Tell me who the fuck sent you, or you die right here and right now." Candice couldn't care less about the gun that rested on her temple.

"Put your gun down and I'll put mine down. We need to talk," Tuck said calmly.

"No! I don't trust you!" she barked, working her jaw and readjusting her grip on her weapon.

"You have no fuckin' choice right now! There are some very dangerous people hunting for your ass, and I'm the only person who can tell you who they are and why they want you dead or alive," Tuck said seriously. "Now put your fuckin' gun down and I'll put mine down," he said firmly.

"You first," Candice said, not buying it. If Tuck tried anything funny, she would take Tuck the fuck apart, limb by limb.

He reluctantly lowered his gun from her head. She took a deep breath and did the same, but she kept it at the ready. Tuck placed his gun back into his waistband as a symbol of trust. He wanted her to know he had no ill intentions toward her.

Candice didn't give a shit what he did. She kept her gun ready, willing and able to blow his skullcap back.

"Now let me explain everything to you," Tuck began with a sigh.

"You already said that bullshit. Start talking . . . and fast. The way I see it right now is you were working for the bastards who killed my family the entire time."

"Candy . . . I was never working for anyone who had anything to do with your family's murders, but I have a lot of information that may be of use to you. I have your father's books—all of his secrets, his life story," Tuck said, his words coming out slowly and deliberately. Candice seemed to soften a bit.

"Where would you get my father's books from if you don't work for the fuckers who killed him?" she asked, her eyebrow raised.

"It's a long story. We don't have time now. I want to show you some of the books and give you a different perspective on your family's past. I want to help you get away from here before you get hurt."

"I can't get sidetracked right now. I will meet you at the Monte Carlo later tonight. You better come alone, or else you die," Candice growled.

"Candy . . . you need to be careful. They are probably watching us right now," Tuck cautioned.

"I'm a big girl. I can handle myself," she said pointedly, reaching for the door handle. Before Tuck could take his next breath, Candice was out of the car and up the street.

Tuck picked up his cell phone to call Carlisle. He needed to gather up all of the files so he could hand them over to Candice.

The phone vibrated in his hand. "Shit!" He jumped, putting his hand over his heart.

"Hello," Tuck barked into the phone.

Ear-shattering screams filtered through the receiver, threatening to burst his eardrums.

"Elaina! What's the matter? What?" Tuck felt his chest heave with effort. He dropped his phone and screeched away from the curb.

"Fuck!" Tuck screamed, taking off like a madman.

They were fucking with the wrong man's family. The game was about to change . . . drastically.

Candice, meanwhile, didn't bother to pull out until she saw Tuck leave, along with his tails. She got out of her car and disappeared down a side street. She dipped into a building before her followers could even get out of their cars.

She watched two men turn down the block, their ties flapping in the wind as they ran from building to building, peeking their heads inside doorways.

After a few minutes the men threw their hands up in exasperation. They were not very diligent in their efforts.

"So fucking impatient and predictable." She smiled.

It was time for her to ramp up the heat on her marks. Candy knew she should have mirked all of them as soon as she gained access to the house. Uncle Rock had told her about becoming personal with her marks; now she had to turn things up. She was back in her hard candy mode.

No man, woman or child would be safe from her wrath.

Chapter 9

Secret Assignations

Guillermo DeSosa took a long pull off his cigarette. His hands shook involuntarily. He paced outside, near the spot he'd agreed on. He looked at his watch impatiently and blew out a thick cloud of smoke. He plucked his cigarette to the ground and began to walk away; his shoulders were slumped in disappointment.

"Did I keep you waiting long?" an effeminate male voice filtered through the crisp night air. The man seemed to materialize from thin air. That shit unnerved Guillermo; he reached for his waistband, jumpy and anxious. He was always on edge with these meetings, especially when he dealt with someone new.

Guillermo kicked himself for answering the Craigslist advertisement. Why didn't he just go his usual route?

"Shit! Don't you know better than to sneak up on a gangster's son?" he huffed, moving his jacket aside so the man could see his shiny piece. He wanted this man to know who would be in charge this evening. He avoided the man's direct gaze; it would be easier this way. They had already discussed through e-mail how things would work. Guillermo wanted to stay low-key, but he disclosed his father's status—just in case the man was thinking about setting him up.

"Pay me first, like we agreed, then tell me where to meet you," the mysterious man said. To an onlooker it appeared as if the two men were not even conversing with one another. Guillermo had a Bluetooth in his ear, and the other man appeared to be texting on his BlackBerry. Neither looked in the other's direction. Guillermo always took precautions in case someone was watching.

"It's all in the envelope," Guillermo said, his voice quavering. He was taking a chance, and he knew it. When his desires took over, all logical thinking evaporated. Walking toward his car, Guillermo quickly placed a small white envelope on top of a black car that was parked three cars away from his.

Guillermo quickly picked up his pace and rushed to his car as if the Furies were on his heels. The man walked swiftly by, swiped the envelope from the car hood, then headed in the opposite direction of Guillermo's car. Guillermo was panting now as blood and adrenaline rushed to his brain. Once inside, he took a deep breath, looked around and pulled away from the curb. After all of these years, the heat of embarrassment still climbed from his chest and settled on his face when he set up these rendezvous. And each time, he felt dirty and ashamed. If his brother and his father knew about his secret lifestyle, he would definitely be excommunicated from the family or—worse—put to sleep like a horse with four broken legs.

The urges had started when Guillermo was just twelve years old; he had felt an overwhelming level of attraction, which he couldn't explain, for members of the same sex. The first time he remembered having a physical response to another boy was in the locker room after gym class. The physical education teacher had entered the locker room and instructed them all to disrobe and jump in the showers after a grueling day of climbing ropes. His friend had dropped his drawers right next to him and casually walked to the showers. As soon as he spied his friend's flaccid penis, he felt himself grow hard.

Guillermo had felt like reaching out and grabbing his friend in his most private area and even kissing him. His friend caught him staring and sent him a look that spoke volumes. Guillermo smiled nervously before running into the bathroom stalls and hiding.

Inside the stall he vomited into the toilet from the shame he felt. He sobbed uncontrollably and wondered what was wrong with him. Why couldn't he be like the other boys, interested in staring at women's breasts and butts? He smacked himself in the head, trying to beat the sordid thoughts out of his own brain.

It hadn't worked, of course. Every day afterward, Guillermo struggled with his identity and unnatural desires, learning to satisfy them in the most discreet ways possible.

When Guillermo spent time with his father and older brother, he acted the consummate ladies' man, even going as far as slapping women's asses in public. He was a wonderful actor and an accomplished liar. Though he often felt like a fraud, he felt these were necessary evils he must carry out to remain a part of the DeSosa family.

Guillermo was Rolando DeSosa's youngest son. He was also DeSosa's illegitimate son; he was the product of his father's well-known philandering. Guillermo's mother was a beautiful young girl who had newly arrived in America from Colombia; then she met Rolando DeSosa. Although he was married, DeSosa just couldn't resist her beautiful dark hair, butter-soft skin and sparkling green eyes. He was twenty-five years her senior when she discovered she was pregnant with his son.

She was the ultimate mistress and played her position well. When she was with DeSosa, she made him feel like he was the only man in the world. When she couldn't be with him due to his family obligations, she held her head high and waited for him to return. She never forced the issue of being number one in DeSosa's life; in turn, he respected her and always took care of her and her son.

DeSosa made sure Guillermo was well cared for as a child, although circumstances didn't allow him to spend as much time with Guillermo as with his legitimate son, Arellio. DeSosa had made sure Guillermo and his mother lived well in a posh New York City condo. He paid tuition for Guillermo's private schools and made sure he had the best of everything.

DeSosa didn't want Guillermo to be in the family business; he had been brutally honest with his son that he didn't believe he had the "heart" to carry out certain business matters. Guillermo had been livid with his father's proclamation and stormed out of his office. He'd gone on a rampage for an entire week. He needed to prove a point to his father.

Guillermo had broken out several windows in his school and set a fire in the school's gymnasium; then he took his rampage to the streets. He'd gotten on a city bus without paying his fare and once inside slapped an innocent woman in the face just for "looking" at him. His wannabe-gangster rampage came to a halt after he stabbed one of his classmates during an altercation, just barely missing the boy's lung.

When DeSosa picked Guillermo up from juvenile hall, he'd calmly asked his son, "You want in so badly, you do all this? Well, you got in. Not because of your stupidity, but because you would go through all of this to be with me . . . to be a part of this family. But you keep doing stupid shit and it will get you killed. Never draw attention to yourself unless it's absolutely necessary."

Everyone in the DeSosa organization knew that Guillermo was soft, so they gave him all of the easy lifting. He sold weight to low-level drug dealers; he attended meetings with his father as a "second gun"; sometimes he rode shotgun with his brother when something slightly dangerous was going down. It suited him just fine. He was probably the most well-paid second-string gangster in New York City.

Guillermo pulled up to the Blake, a small hotel situated on a side street, out of the glaring New York City lights. He'd already picked up his room keys earlier in the day; the second key lay in the hands of his new prospect, nestled carefully in the envelope.

Inside the hotel lobby Guillermo looked around suspiciously. He nodded at the front-desk clerk, who stared at him a bit too long and hard. Guillermo always wondered if people recognized him as readily as they did his father and his brother.

The elevator seemed to take forever to get to the sixth floor. The familiar *ding* as the doors eased open was like music to his ears. Guillermo rushed out, but then he slowed his pace, not wanting to appear too eager. The hallway was a like a ghost town. He exhaled a sigh of relief; he hated seeing people milling about the halls. He always felt paranoid about running into one of his father's acquaintances, or meeting a set of judgmental eyes.

With trembling hands Guillermo used his key to enter the room. No matter how many times he did this, he was nervous all over again. It was dark inside. The only light came from a small candle, which was on the nightstand. He smirked to himself.

"You trying to be romantic?" he called out as he shrugged out of his leather jacket. There was no answer. Guillermo tossed his jacket aside and moved farther into the room.

"C'mon, I don't like playing games," he called out.

Frustration and anxiety could be heard in his voice. He felt spooked by the dim lighting, so he reached over and flicked on a light. His boy toy must be getting ready in the bathroom. Guillermo didn't like waiting for anyone or anything, especially not after he'd been so long without a man.

"I'm taking off my clothes, which means get your ass out here and give me what the fuck I paid for," he barked as he unbuckled his pants and stepped out of them. He figured his little plaything was playing hide the dick in the bathroom. Guillermo wasn't much for games. He planned to bust in that damn bathroom and shock the little punk-ass guy with a stiff dick in the ass. Guillermo stomped over to the bathroom door.

"You like to play these kinky games? Well, I'm going to show you who can do it best," he called out, using one hand to rub his flaccid dick. He wanted to be ready to pound into that ass.

Guillermo snatched the bathroom door open, intending to surprise his date with his rock hard dick. Guillermo's mouth dropped open and his eyes threatened to pop out of their socket. His dick instantly went limp and his bladder released itself.

"What the—" Guillermo had started to speak, but then put his hands up in front of him defensively. It was too late. He had nowhere to run, nowhere to hide. He was half naked and completely defenseless without his weapon.

"P—please," he managed to stammer out, but his words died in the air. He screamed like a bitch as he came face-to-face with the devil. He fell to the ground, feeling the cold porcelain tiles on his back. He could taste his own blood pooling in his mouth. Suddenly Guillermo's vision faded and his world went completely black.

Elaina barreled into Avon's chest like a bulldozer as he walked through the front door of her mother's house. He let out a puff of air and stumbled backward, caught off guard. She was sobbing, her body shaking uncontrollably.

"Shh," he comforted, wrapping his arms around her protectively. He held her tightly for a few minutes and stroked the top of her head. Her body eased into his embrace and she seemed to calm down significantly in his arms.

Avon pulled her away from his chest so he could look at her face to make sure she wasn't hurt. Her face was blotchy and red from crying, but beautiful nonetheless. He felt his heart thump in his chest. At that moment he didn't care about the past, about her betrayal or the affair. Despite all that they had been through, he still loved his wife.

"Elaina, tell me what happened," Avon said softly, gazing into her eyes.

"They—they . . . shot . . . Pfeiffer and the car. We had just gotten out. . . . They just missed me, the kids . . . oh my God!" she cried, collapsing back onto her husband's chest.

"What! Who?" Avon gasped. He felt like the air had been squeezed out of his lungs. They had come after his family, after all. He was livid, beyond rage.

"I don't know who! The gunshots were so loud! They hit the car like hail pellets. I screamed and grabbed the kids. We had just pulled into the driveway. Then . . . then Pfeiffer fell. He was bleeding all over the place. We pulled him inside the garage . . . but . . . he—he's dead!" She cried some more, her body quaking all over.

Avon flexed his jaw and hugged her even tighter now. His world was spinning off its axis. He couldn't believe Stokes actually came after his family like he'd threatened. This shit meant war.

Avon let Elaina go and started for the garage. His nostrils flared so hard that he thought he'd hyperventilate. He gritted his teeth and lifted his forearm over his nose at the unbecoming smell in the air. The metallic raw meat smell of blood threatened to make him hurl. He stepped over the dead dog and looked at the car. He surveyed the damage and surmised that the holes were made with a high-powered semiautomatic weapon.

Avon slammed his fists on the hood of his wife's car. He could feel adrenaline pulsing through his veins, fast and hot.

"We need to call the police," Elaina said from the doorway. She interrupted Avon's murderous thoughts.

He looked at her, with fire flashing in his eyes. His hands were balled into knuckle-paling fists. "No, we are not going to call the local police. They won't do shit but bring more attention to the house. I will find out what happened. I will protect you and my kids, Elaina," he assured her, pinching the bridge of his nose.

"Where are the kids?" he asked, noticing the unusual silence in the house for the first time. "Where did you send my kids?" he persisted, stalking toward his trembling wife.

Elaina threw her hands up in the air. Her mouth was open, but no words were coming out. She seemed to be melting down before his eyes. Her mother in the backdrop scowling did not help the situation.

"Elaina! Where are my fuckin' kids?" Avon snapped, shaking her shoulders roughly. Panic was choking him around the throat.

"Oh God!" she cried, knocking his hands away, as if she were a victim of domestic violence.

Avon removed his hands from her person as if she were a hot stove that had just burned him.

"Elaina, I'm sorry. Please . . . tell me where the kids are." He softened his tone, moving a few steps away from her. His heart hammered against his chest bone.

Avon had never wanted to be the person to make her afraid again. They'd had their ups and downs, especially when the accidental shooting had threatened to bring his DEA career to a halt. Unfortunately, on a few occasions when he had been extremely stressed with the job, Avon had unwittingly taken his anger out on Elaina, slapping her across the face.

It had been one of Avon's lowest personal moments as a husband, and there was no turning back the hands of time. Avon apologized profusely after each incident, but his wife had clearly grown weary of his moods and his unpredictable bursts of anger.

Avon grabbed his bald head and squeezed it, trying to calm himself down. He took a deep breath and put his hands out in front of his chest. He would be calm and reasonable with his wife.

"Baby, I'm not going to be angry. Just tell me where they are so I can protect all of you." He steadied his voice, letting his anger subside like a flame smothered in dirt.

"I have them hiding in a closet downstairs," she finally admitted, hanging her head as if she were the worst mother in the world. Relief washed over Avon; at least she hadn't done anything drastic or stupid. "Avon, I was scared. That's why I put them there." She seemed to be stumbling in explanation.

He placed his finger against her lips. "Hush, you don't need to explain, I understand," he whispered, the words catching in his throat.

Elaina lifted her head; her eyes pleaded with him for answers. "Avon, tell me what is going on? Who is after you? Who would do this to us?" She searched his eyes, his face, for answers from her estranged husband.

Avon didn't respond. He didn't have the words. His own mind raced. He brushed past her and rushed from the garage back into the house. He ran over to the basement door and yanked it open; he rushed down the dark stairwell to free his children from their confinement.

He found his kids huddled together in the corner of the closet. The sight of them cowering in fear sent a pang of hurt through Avon's stomach. His daughter was crying as she held her brother in a death grip, like he was her life raft. His son sat in urine-soaked pants. The sight broke Avon's heart. Tears burned at the back of his eyes as he knelt down and scooped them both up into his strong arms. He needed them to know he would never let anything happen to them . . . ever.

"C'mere. Daddy is here now," Avon whispered, the heat of his breath on his daughter's face, a soothing balm to her tears.

She immediately buried her face in her father's neck and sobbed, just like her mother had done a few minutes earlier. His son was another story. The boy's sweat-and-piss-drenched body hung in Avon's arms, stiff and stoic. He didn't bend or respond to his father's soft words. Instead, the boy stared right past his father's face and looked off into the distance, at nothing. The boy was scared shitless. One tear streaked, unchecked, down his cheek.

"You guys okay?" Avon whispered, kissing both of them on the forehead. He had to make sure his children didn't see how angry or terrified he truly felt.

"Daddy, somebody shot Pfeiffer!" his daughter wailed. Her little voice quavered with fear. "Oh, baby, I know. I know. I'm so sorry Daddy wasn't here. I'll never let anything like this happen again. I promise," he comforted, meaning every word. His son didn't say a word and still had not responded to his presence. He just stared blankly above his head. Avon shook him and tried to get him to talk. The boy was still in shock.

"Fuck," Avon huffed under his breath. There would be fucking hell to pay when he found the bastards who had shot at his family. Avon was taking off the kid gloves and going full-metal jacket with these pricks.

He took the kids back upstairs to their rooms. There was no way he would allow them to stay in a closet like scared puppies.

When his mother-in-law came home, her face was dark and her body stiffened at the sight of Avon. Helen held on to her daughter like she was a treasure beyond worth.

When he moved closer to Elaina, she tightened her grip, turning her face up at him as if he were a smelly skunk. There was really nothing he could say to comfort a woman who had come so close to losing her daughter and grandkids within the blink of an eye. Despite her resistance, Avon needed to make some quick and hard decisions that involved Helen's acquiescence.

"We all have to leave here," Avon announced seriously.

Elaina looked up in surprise and fear. Helen looked
at him like he'd lost his damn mind. She stared at him
with coldly hooded eyes.

"No! We need to call the police and get to the bottom of this! You can't keep coming here with all of
your secrets and spy games, putting my daughter and
grandkids in danger!" His mother-in-law lit into him.
She was on her feet now, standing toe-to-toe with Avon
like a lioness protecting her pride.

He felt her pain, but he also felt his cheeks go flush
with anger. It didn't matter how long he'd been gone
in the past and what mistakes he'd made, he was the
head of his family. Avon ground his back teeth together
and composed himself. He jutted his finger toward his
mother-in-law and squinted his eyes.

"You can stay here, but my wife and kids are coming
with me!" Avon countered. He looked at his wife expectantly; when she didn't follow his lead, he grabbed both
of his kids by their hands and ushered them toward the
front door.

Elaina got up reluctantly and looked at her mother
with tear-filled eyes. She was so torn; it was all too
much to process.

"You have to come with us, Mama. It's not safe here,"
she begged. Her mother pursed her lips and wrangled
her arm away from her daughter's desperate grasp.

"It's not safe where he is either," her mother replied,
folding her arms across her chest, refusing to leave her
home.

Elaina gave her mother a desperate look, but she
knew it was useless. In the end, like a dutiful wife and
mother, she followed her husband and kids out of the
house.

All she could do now was pray that her mother would be safe. That's all she could do for all of them—pray that they would be safe.

"Ma! Ma!" Junior called out in a state of panic as he rushed back into his SoHo apartment. He was sweating profusely and his legs shook. The apartment was not big; so when Betty didn't answer, Junior's stomach began to cramp.

"Ma?" he belted out again, his voice cracking with desperation. Then he heard the water running from behind the bathroom door. He rushed to the door and knocked, hoping that his mother simply hadn't heard him over the rush of the running faucet.

"Ma!" he called out again, twisting the doorknob. Now was not the time for him to worry about invading her privacy. The door gave easily. The shower was running, but the curtain was pulled closed. Junior reached out and snatched back the curtain.

"Oh shit!" he huffed. Those were the last words he spoke before his world went black.

A black hood had been forcefully placed over his head, snatching his breath away. A sharp pain invaded his spine and his legs buckled. His body went limp; his legs betrayed him as he fought against his own body to stay standing. Junior knew falling was the kiss of death; yet it was the inevitable. His back hit the marble tile floor, sending a spine-crushing pain through his back and down his legs. Junior opened his mouth to scream, but the sound was stuck in the back of his throat. Instead, he took in a mouthful of black fibers from the hood, which scratched the back of his throat. He was being dragged now; his legs flip-flopping like a fish out of water.

Something crashed into his diaphragm. Vomit involuntarily spewed up from his stomach and into the black sackcloth. His hands clawed at the edges of the material, which threatened to cut off his air supply. His esophagus was being crushed; he felt tiny needles creeping up his body from his feet. Junior knew that meant he was drifting away, losing consciousness. The thought caused him to fight harder.

His assailant's communications sounded like muffled, hushed whispers in his obstructed ears. A crushing blow to the face caused something to explode behind Junior's eyes. He could feel the moisture seeping into his death hood from his busted face. A kick in the nuts sent a shock wave of pain through his entire body. He reacted as if someone had put him in an electric chair, his body seizing and jerking violently.

Junior couldn't hold on for much longer. He could see Broady's face like a painting on his eyelids. Then his mother's face—the last vision of it, contorted, stiff, came into focus. Another hit to the body brought Junior back momentarily.

"You fucked with the wrong ones, nigga!" he heard, barely making out the choppy voices. He didn't know if it was the hood or the fact that his ears were ringing. He was dragged to a new spot on the floor; the carpet was burning his back. More punches, kicks and boot stomps rained down on his body.

"Don't kill him! The boss wants him alive," one of his assailants said before he laid his fist into Junior's gut for good measure.

Junior was transported from one black world into another.

Chapter 10

Upping the Ante

Candice rushed through the familiar doors of the shooting range. Her heart immediately sank. She missed her uncle at times like these. In fact, she had been thinking about him a lot lately. Candice wondered what he'd think about her current predicament.

"Candy, you can't be a cleaner and be so emotional," he'd tell her.

The range was a place of solace for her. The smell of lead, the sound of bullets flying and the power she felt when she shot her weapons helped alleviate much of her stress. Also, she needed to sharpen her skills a bit.

She was only fifteen years old when she came to the firing range the first time. The adrenaline that had coursed through her veins that first day had caused her knees to knock and her stomach to churn. Uncle Rock had told her to relax and focus on the task—getting her shots down range, on target and stopping the threat.

Yes, stopping the threat had always been her mission.

Uncle Rock had stepped up behind her that day and instructed her to pick up the first gun she'd ever held—a .40-caliber Glock 22. The rough handle felt comforting against the palms of her hand. She felt like a superhero when she held the metal beauty.

"Grip and trigger pull are the most important aspects to shooting, Candy," Uncle Rock had told her. He'd placed her hands in the correct position and let her dry fire the weapon. When she did it the first time, she jerked the trigger.

"You're anticipating the shot. Let every shot be a surprise," he urged, trying to ease her nervousness.

Candice had never seen Uncle Rock so passionate about anything, so in tune with the weapon and with his pupil.

When he thought she was ready, Uncle Rock had inserted the magazine into the weapon. "It's your time to shine, Candy Cane," Uncle Rock announced like a proud father.

His words of encouragement made her feel warm inside, just like when her father used to call her Candy Cane. Candice's first five shots were dead center mass.

Today Candice swallowed the lump that had formed at the back of her throat and shook off those haunting memories. She couldn't let her emotions take control, not now.

She looked down at the other range stalls; three were occupied by men. None of them were paying her any attention. *Good.* She rolled the bright orange foam earplugs between her fingers until they were small enough to fit into her ear canals. She smiled as she remembered Uncle Rock's voice instructing her to "always double bag your ears or you'll be like me, a deaf and dumb old man."

It was a cheesy joke, but it always made her giggle. Occasionally he would even crack a rare smile over the comment.

She plugged her ears with hard ear protection and slid her specialized clear plastic protective eye goggles over her eyes. The black gloves were the last step.

She worked her fingers into the leather gloves; she hated shooting with gloves because it made getting her rounds on target and in the five rings a bit more of a challenge. But Uncle Rock warned her hundreds of times about the dangers of lead particles getting all over her hands, contaminating her skin and blood.

Candice set her jaw and stomped her left foot, angry at herself for getting all mushy. Candice swiveled her neck and cracked her knuckles. She needed to toughen up for this war. "This is all for you, Daddy. Uncle Rock, I'm going to make you proud. I'm going to do everything right this time," she whispered to herself.

The sound of rounds being fired from the adjacent shooting lanes gave Candice the push that she needed. She pulled down the gun rest and placed her perfect plastic case on it. The handmade case had been created by Uncle Rock to house what Candice considered the best gift she had ever received. Candice slowly unlatched the case and pulled up the top in a dramatic fashion, as if unveiling the Hope Diamond. When the case flapped open, Candice's eyes sparkled and she smiled down at her uncle's gift. The feeling of excitement that Uncle Rock's beautiful AR-15 had given her many years ago was even stronger today.

Candice moved to the left and put the weapon on her support-side shoulder. She blew out a cleansing breath and tried to relax. She closed her eyes for a few seconds and imagined Uncle Rock guiding her movements. She placed her support-side ear on her shoulder.

"Candy, you gotta get your head down behind the sights or else this will jump back and hit you in the face. Grip it here, like your life depended on it. C'mon, Candy, now take this. Get your head behind those sights. Get a firm grasp and learn how to treat this baby like it's your own." Uncle Rock's voice guided her from the grave and beyond.

Candice let her legs go soft and bent her knees slightly, with her back straight. She got into the correct stance and positioned the gun properly. Closing her weak eye and keeping her dominant eye open, Candice tugged on the trigger. When the first couple of rounds exited the end of the gun in rapid fire, Candice looked down range at the ripped-up target. She carefully pulled the trigger back again and again. Finally she was satisfied as she called in the obliterated target.

"Well, DeSosa, you better be fuckin' ready because your time has run out." Candice didn't care who heard her or who watched her. She was completely in her element, and single-minded in her objective.

Arellio DeSosa opened the strange manila envelope left on his car windshield. He read the strange writing on the front. It was his name spelled out in letters that were cut out from magazines and newspapers. Curious, he turned the envelope over and dumped out its contents.

Arellio doubled over like he'd taken a powerful gut punch. His heartbeat sped up; his hands were racked with tremors. He looked at graphic 8X10 glossy photographs. He frantically flipped through them; each one was worse than the previous one. Finally he arrived at the last picture.

"No!" Arellio let out a guttural scream, dropping all of the pictures to the ground. Cyndi came rushing out the front door and down the long, circular driveway. She found her husband sitting on the ground next to his car, sobbing like a woman. He shouted "No! No! No!" over and over again. A cold chill shook Cyndi to the core. Something very bad had gone down.

"Arellio? What is it?" she asked, touching him on the head. She quickly discovered his source of distress. Cyndi went to her knees to retrieve the scattered photographs. Her chest tightened and tears burned behind her eyes. She picked up the photographs and was overcome with a mixture of grief and disbelief.

The first photo depicted her brother-in-law, Guillermo, with his head thrown back and eyes closed as another man took in a mouthful of his manhood. Cyndi felt sick as vomit crept up her throat.

With her eyes wide she shuffled to the next picture. "Oh God!" she gasped. It was a frontal shot of Guillermo, his face clear as day. He was on his knees, a man mounting him from behind. Guillermo's face seemed contorted—whether in pain or pleasure, Cyndi could not tell. She felt light-headed. How could she comfort her husband through this disgrace?

The next picture showed Guillermo picking up a man and handing him money on a dark street corner.

The following picture felled her completely. Guillermo had a look of pure shock and terror on his face. His eyes bulged almost out of his head, and his mouth hung open in a terrified O shape. A severed penis was shoved between his lips.

Cyndi let out a loud screech. If this had been some kind of nightmare, she would have hoped she'd wake up soon. With trembling hands she flipped to the last picture in the stack. Cyndi twisted her body away from her husband and vomited on the driveway. The eviscerated remains of her brother-in-law were too much for herself and her husband to handle. How could they offer comfort to one another when they both were in so much pain?

***

"You motherfucker!" Tucker boomed, rushing toward the old man, spit flying from his mouth. "You fucked with my family? I'm going to rip your fucking head off and shit down your neck, you old bastard!"

Three black suits stepped in Tucker's path, forming a wall around their charge. Grayson Stokes didn't even flinch, his icy eyes remaining steady and calm. He folded his wrinkled hands on the table in front of him like he was watching a boring variety show rerun.

Avon struggled against a wall of muscles. "I'm gonna kill you! Fuckin' white devil!" he barked. The walls of the room felt like they were closing in on him. "Face me like a man!" Avon challenged.

"Is that why you asked to meet me, Agent Tucker? So you could curse at me? So you could make yourself look like a total fool?" Stokes said calmly in his throaty, phlegm-coated voice.

"No, I asked to meet you so I could fucking kill you, you piece of shit! What type of fucking games are you playing?" Tucker could barely contain his anger. Veins throbbed at his temple and in his neck. He felt like he was having an "Incredible Hulk" moment.

"What makes you think it was me that tried to harm your family, Agent Tucker?" Stokes asked, peering around the broad backs of his protectors. "Do you really think you are that important to me?"

"Who else would do it? Who else would have a reason to do it?" Tucker contorted his jaw so hard he gave himself a headache.

"Did you ever think that DeSosa would do something like that? He is a fucking criminal, Agent Tucker. He knows you were undercover, infiltrating his top drug-dealing thug. Don't you think he has a reason to go after your family?" Stokes painted these scenarios for him to make him think twice about his current conspiracy theory.

"DeSosa wouldn't even know where to find my family!" Tucker boomed, jutting a trembling finger at Stokes. Stokes chortled and then was overcome with a fit of coughing.

Tucker felt like he'd been bitch slapped by Stokes. His patience snapped. Tucker bulldozed into the three Stokes protectors. "You think it's funny, you half-dead motherfucker!" he screamed as he dived across the table with his hands outstretched.

He wasn't fast enough. He was roughhoused by the suits and put into an arm bar, his arms raised over his head and locked behind his neck. The pain that rushed down his spine as a result rendered Tucker helpless. He had no choice but to calm down. Breathing like a captured animal, he finally stopped flailing and fighting.

With a deadpan expression Stokes watched Tucker's face; the old man's demeanor was as calm as a placid river. Finally he waved his right hand in the air like it was a magic wand. "That's enough," he called out, snapping his fingers as though calling off well-trained attack dogs.

Tucker was released. He collapsed onto a chair and waited for the feeling to come back into his arms.

"Another hotheaded Tucker." Stokes shook his head in disappointment, as though Tucker was simply a lazy student who didn't do his homework.

Tucker was back on alert; his eyes were hooded over with ill intent.

"You think I didn't know about your hero daddy? Agent Tucker, I know everything. But do you? I bet you didn't know your father *wasn't really* the undercover narcotics detective shot dead in a buy and bust," Stokes said cruelly.

"You shut the fuck up!" Tucker growled. His teeth were clenched together tightly; his words were barely audible.

"Your father was no more than a dirty drug cop who was taking payments from drug dealers. He got shot because he wanted out—just like Easy Hardaway. He wanted to get into a game he knew nothing about, and there was no turning back. There's never a way out, only a fucking way in, A-gent Tu-cker!" Stokes spoke like a preacher in the pulpit; his eyes were dilated and flashing with malice.

Tucker shot up out of the chair. He was faster this time and managed to catch Stokes around his frail turkey neck. Tucker squeezed as hard as he could from across the table. "You're a fuckin' liar! I'm gonna kill you, once and for all!" Tucker howled, snot pouring from his nose. His brain felt as if it would burst through his skull with all of the pressure building inside his head.

The men in black were on him in a matter of seconds. He held on as if his life depended on it. Stokes was making a horrible rasping noise, like a grating car engine that wouldn't turn over.

"Die!" Tucker hissed.

Finally the men were able to pry him off Stokes. His body shook with angry tremors. Tucker was forced back down onto his chair. He held his head in his hands, while his chest rose and fell rapidly.

Stokes was ruining his life and tainting the memory of his father. Nothing in his life was off-limits. Everything that was holy and sacred had been desecrated by this bastard.

When Tucker was ten years old, the New York City chief of police had handed him a folded American flag amid a bevy of flashing camera lights. Avon had felt a mix of emotions—grief and pride, anger and disbelief. He held the triangularly folded flag against his small chest; it was the flag that had been removed from the top of his father's mahogany casket. A twenty-one-gun salute followed; this was the norm for an officer who had been killed in the line of duty.

Avon remembered how the sun had burned his eyes as he tried to look up at his mother's wet face. Her body was shaking with sobs as a chunky, older woman belted out a soul-stirring rendition of "Amazing Grace." Holding his flag with one arm, Avon reached out and grabbed his mother's hand. A wet, crumpled piece of tissue clutched in her palm prevented the skin-to-skin contact that Avon craved. Nonetheless, he would settle for any sort of comfort at this point. He squeezed her hand tightly and closed his eyes. He wanted to see his father one more time.

Avon always liked the way his father's gun looked holstered at his side with his belt badge shining in front. He had always felt a sense of pride when his father came home with yet another police award for valor. Avon even remembered his father once pinning his NYPD police lapel pin to his Easter Sunday suit.

He hated having those memories sullied by Stokes.

Stokes coughed through his maniacal laughter. "Now, Agent Tucker, are you ready to hear everything? Are you ready to talk so we can work together to find the girl and protect your family?" Stokes asked.

They appeared to be back at square one.

With his chest heaving and nostrils flaring, Tucker narrowed his eyes and glared at Stokes. He would at least hear him out. If it involved his family, there was nothing he wouldn't do to protect them.

"All right, then. Now that I have your full attention, let me start from the very beginning," Stokes said, sliding a file in Tucker's direction. "I know you've already seen these, but you only have the Hardaway files. I don't think you know much about Joseph Barton or Rolando DeSosa . . . or the government for that matter," Stokes said.

"I don't wanna read any more of your fuckin' lies! Be a man. Tell me the truth, eye to fucking eye! Tell me how you manipulated a man into selling drugs that poisoned his own fuckin' people. Tell me how the fuckin' government sells drugs to buy weapons for fuckin' militants in other countries. . . . Yeah, tell me!" Tucker growled. He wanted Grayson Stokes to know he was not on his side now, and he never would be a part of his fucking games.

"All right, then, Agent Tucker, I can do that. But you have to be able to handle the truth," Stokes replied. The old man then steepled his fingers together, allowing the pad of each digit to match with its counterpart on the opposite hand. Stokes began to narrate, cleansing himself of it all and taking Tucker on a journey through the past.

He might hate Stokes's guts, but this was exactly the kind of information Tucker needed to help Candy.

Chapter 11

Players and Traitors

New York 1984

"Hit him again," Grayson Stokes growled, circling the victim like a buzzard over a dead body.

Stokes possessed the body of a U.S. Marine and the face of a Calvin Klein model; yet he was as ruthless as a black widow spider. His new mission had come directly from the director of the Central Intelligence Agency—an honor for an agent as high as being knighted by the queen of England.

At his direction a huge gorilla-shaped man approached. The man's meaty hands held the opposing ends of two battery cables; the clamps squeezed open like the hungry mouth of a shark. Stokes nodded at the man, giving him the signal.

Without any facial emotion the man roughly clipped the menacing metal clamps onto the victim's exposed nipples.

The other man fiddled with a box; soon there was a crackling electric sound, like an old transistor radio. Guttural screams emerged from the victim's diaphragm and echoed off the walls. Stokes rubbed his chin, contemplating his next move.

"Rolando DeSosa . . . the Dominican kingpin of New York City," Stokes said sarcastically, circling again. "Are you going to tell me to go fuck myself again, *or are you going to get with the program?" Stokes pushed DeSosa's suspended body, causing it to swing like he was a slab of meat in a butcher shop.*

DeSosa's body was racked with tremors; he was a far cry from the cocky, slick-talking Tony Montana– wannabe who had strode into the room earlier.

"Fuck you," DeSosa rasped, his throat feeling like he'd swallowed acid.

Stokes's eyebrows arched high at DeSosa's bravado. "Fuck me, huh?" Stokes laughed. Then his smile faded as fast as it had formed. Stokes quickly nodded to his henchmen. One of the suited thugs came forward with a scalpel.

DeSosa moaned. There was only so much pain a man could tolerate in his lifetime. "No, no, no," he mumbled, his battered eyes assessed the torture tool. His mind was barely able to comprehend the cruel trick that fate had played on him, for surely he would suffer dearly for his sins before he died.

The thugs made several small incisions on DeSosa's chest, like tribal initiation markings. Then they poured salt and alcohol onto it. DeSosa didn't have any sound left in his voice box; his mouth just hung open in sheer terror.

Stokes turned his back, anxiously rubbing his fingernails on the breast of his suit. He closed his eyes as DeSosa finally got enough wind in his lungs to let out a bloodcurdling scream.

"Now, Rolando. Again, let me tell you who I am. Maybe your English is not too good, so you didn't understand me the first time. I work for President Ronald Reagan. You do know who that is, right? He's the man who allowed scum like you to enter our country, only to find out that you came here to get rich by selling drugs," Stokes said condescendingly, addressing the top of DeSosa's downturned head.

DeSosa couldn't and wouldn't dare answer. He'd had enough.

With the flick of his hand, Stokes's people were pulling DeSosa down from the chains and relocating him to a cold metal chair. His head was fighting a major battle with his neck; eventually it lobbed forward until his chin hit his chest. Stokes stood menacingly in front of him.

"You feel better sitting on the chair?" Stokes continued, not giving DeSosa a chance to even respond. "So, now, this little thing we want you to agree to. It's sort of like an immunity deal. We take you out of prison. We give you access to the newest spin on cocaine, and you do our good president a favor by finding the right people in the worst neighborhoods to distribute this new phenomenal wonder drug—which we call crack cocaine—to. You following me, DeSosa?"

Stokes grabbed a handful of DeSosa's thick, dark hair so that he could look him directly in the eye. DeSosa could barely keep his battered eyelids open long enough to stare back.

"Rolando, I have about twelve more ways to make you say yes. Why don't we avoid using those methods? All you need to do is just open your mouth and repeat after me: 'I, Rolando DeSosa, will agree to help this great country of the United States, which allowed my cockroach spic ass to come here and make money off its people,'" Stokes dictated. "Or should we start with that machine right there? I believe it does something permanent. Tell me, how much do you value your eyesight, Rolando?" Stokes threatened in a maddeningly calm tone.

DeSosa still did not acquiesce right away; instead, it took four more methods of torture before he finally cracked. In the end he agreed to the CIA's program to distribute crack cocaine in low-income neighborhoods in New York City and Los Angeles.

At the time no one, not even the CIA, knew the distribution was being used to fund Reagan's Contras. Stokes had only agreed to the program because he was told that controlling the distribution of this new and cheap spin on regular cocaine would help the government rid its country of the worst ghettos, like a self-inflicted genocide.

Stokes had signed on because he was a loyal employee of the government. He had thrown his moral compass in the trash compartment many years ago, and had no intention of retrieving it anytime soon.

Easy Hardaway was recruited into Operation Easy In, after his name had been passed to DeSosa by an NYPD detective named Francis Moore. Francis Moore was a decorated police hero; he was a rising rank-and-file detective, street legend and hard-nosed narc, who had put the worst of the worst behind bars for life.

Rolando DeSosa knew Moore differently. He knew Moore as the dirty detective he had kept on his payroll for years. Their relationship had proved very beneficial to DeSosa. Each and every time he had a run-in with the NYPD, his name would be cleared; then he'd be back on the street in a matter of days, and sometimes hours, thanks to Moore's diligent work.

Until Moore's only daughter, Corine, had begun dating a scraggly street kid known to every cop and detective as Easy, his life had been pretty uncomplicated. As the protégé of Early, a longtime criminal, Moore naturally had concerns about the safety of Corine in the presence of Easy.

One night Moore stormed into DeSosa's hangout spot in Harlem, sweating and visibly upset. He had been searching for DeSosa for days. He needed DeSosa to take care of his little "problem." But clearly, DeSosa had problems of his own.

"What the hell happened to you?" Moore asked, noticing the healing cuts and bruises on DeSosa's face, neck and hands.

DeSosa had waved off the questions. "What is it that you want from me, Detective Moore? I haven't been out there, so I don't have anything for you."

"What makes you think I want something?" Moore asked defensively.

DeSosa raised an arrogant eyebrow. "Because dirty cops only come around when they want something."

Moore explained the situation with his daughter. He believed Eric Hardaway to be a no-good street thug who had stolen his daughter away from him and his wife.

DeSosa dismissed Moore's paternal concerns, at first. "I'm not doing jur fuckin' dirty work. You have a personal vendetta against the kid, ju handle it," DeSosa said dismissively.

Moore was his employee, not the other way around. DeSosa didn't fucking have time for this personal bullshit—what with the government breathing down his back.

Moore, however, persisted like a bulldog with a bone. He simply knew that if Easy Hardaway stayed romantically involved with his daughter, Corine would end up dead in a back alley. It simply wasn't a risk he was willing to take.

Exasperated, DeSosa heard Moore out, but he considered a different course of action. Why kill a perfectly good drug dealer? The instruction Stokes pro-

vided to DeSosa was to recruit specific types of people for the program—poor people, illiterates, high-school dropouts. These recruits also needed to be hungry for fast money and posses a work ethic strong enough to generate a decent cash flow.

Easy, in many ways, was a highly qualified candidate for the program. Easy was like a wrapped Christmas gift that had been left under the tree for DeSosa.

Moore gave DeSosa information about Easy's last whereabouts, as well as his street affiliations, daily routine, known accomplices, etc. He had done all of the legwork, which meant all DeSosa had to do was track him down and make him an offer he couldn't refuse.

Easy was a kid coming up on the street, making a name for himself; he was known to many for being the quiet kid who ran in silence and violence. Easy was always hungry for his next dollar. He beat the block, day in and day out. He worked tirelessly at his job and was very smart at evading the police radar. No matter how many times they tried to snag him, Easy had strategically avoided detention and arrest. If the cops thought they had enough probable cause to do a "stop and frisk" of Easy's car, they never found what they were looking for, because there was never enough evidence to haul his ass off to jail.

Easy was smart about his hustle; he knew Early would have been proud of the name he had worked hard building for himself. Easy became especially careful in his dealings, however, after falling in love with and impregnating the daughter of a cop. He didn't want to jeopardize his newfound family by making rookie mistakes. Now his main responsibility was feeding the unborn children who grew in his girl's belly and protecting them all from harm.

DeSosa sent a man with a message for Easy. "Ro-lando DeSosa, the biggest kingpin in New York, wants to see you. He heard about how hard you work out here on these streets, and he wants you to come and talk to him. He wants you to move fuckin' weight for him."

Always the skeptic, Easy didn't take the guy very seriously. In fact, Easy looked the little Hispanic dude up and down, scowling, and said, "Get the fuck outta here with that fantasy bullshit. Y'all niggas always tryin'a set a nigga up. A nigga like me been on these streets for a minute. I was born at night, nigga, not last night!" The small man scampered away like a dog with his tail caught between his legs.

After that encounter Easy stepped up his arsenal of weapons, strategically placing them at home, in his car and on his person. He didn't trust a damn soul anymore.

It wasn't until DeSosa sent his own men, and not a street flunky, to deliver the message personally to Easy that he even considered the possibility of working for DeSosa.

He had spotted them walking feverishly toward him from a heavily tinted car. Easy was an the high ready, reaching for his waistband, but they responded by opening their trench coats and showing their bare waistbands. With hands raised in peace, one guapo boomed, "We bring a message from our boss."

Still wary of their presence in his territory, Easy kept a safe distance from them. DeSosa really wanted to see him; this was the general song the honchos were singing.

Easy had some questions that needed answering first. "Little ol' me? Why me? Of all the hustlin' dudes in BK . . . why me?"

The men assured him that all of his questions would be answered when he met with their boss.

Though Easy was flattered by the offer, he worried that he was being set up. Perhaps DeSosa wanted to get rid of all the competition and expand his own enterprise. Everyone knew DeSosa—he was the man pushing the fast-moving cocaine, which not only cost less than other street drugs, but brought in more profit by sheer volume of sales than heroin or weed could ever net.

After two sleepless nights of weighing the pros and cons of doing business with DeSosa, Easy finally had decided he would strap up and at least meet the man in person. He would hear the man out; and if DeSosa even hinted at taking over Easy's spots, the meeting would be over before the shit even started.

In the meantime, Easy remained cautious with whom he shared his news. He knew better than to blab his mouth to any of the jealous dudes he worked around on the streets. In fact, there was only one person Easy trusted, aside from Corine, and that was Rock Barton.

Easy appeared in DeSosa's Spanish Harlem club office. His baby face was clear of blemishes, wrinkles or worry. The budding goatee he grew was the only indication that he was even old enough to drive. Easy stood a gangly six foot two inches; his rail-thin frame was covered in his best digs. He was decked out in a butter-soft leather blazer, cashmere mock neck sweater, Potenza slacks and his first pair of suede Salvatore Ferragamo loafers. A lone gold crucifix with a ruby crown at the top sat in the middle of Easy's chest, a diamond pinkie ring graced his left pinkie. His gaudy way of dressing screamed drug dealer or pimp. This was something his friend Rock had been lecturing him to change lately.

"Sit down, Easy," DeSosa instructed in his thick accent.

Easy nodded respectfully and took a seat. Easy's heart hammered and his palms were soaking wet. He splayed them open, flat on his pants legs, and rubbed them dry.

DeSosa's style was simple. No jewelry, no flashy clothes, just a very regal presence that said, I'm in charge. DeSosa stubbed out his customary cigar and leveled Easy with a look.

"I selected you for my own reasons," DeSosa began. He bombarded Easy with a series of questions; within an hour they were speaking fluidly and comfortably.

Easy felt a great amount of respect for DeSosa. He felt like DeSosa was a kindred spirit, someone whom Easy had known his entire life. Easy and DeSosa built their relationship on mutual respect and on a common goal—getting rich fast.

DeSosa educated Easy on the business of marketing mass quantities of crack cocaine at prices that would guarantee sales at lightning speed. In weeks Easy became the man to see in Brooklyn. Everybody knew he was pushing weight and he was offering a fair price for his product. Soon Easy's drug operation grew, and he became one of the biggest crack cocaine distributors in New York City.

Rolando DeSosa was his lone supplier. It was like a match made in heaven. At first, Easy was just getting eight ounces or so at a time, worth about $15,000. But as Easy's drug empire expanded, he began putting in orders for kilos' worth of crack cocaine, worth tens of millions of dollars. Easy never asked DeSosa any questions about his access to such vast quantities of product. That was one of the reasons his relationship with DeSosa worked so well. DeSosa did the supply-

ing and Easy met the demands on the street—no questions asked.

Before long, Easy became a certified kingpin, with over a dozen crack houses in Brooklyn, churning out $30,000 to $50,000 a day in profits. His network of drug dealers sold so many crack rocks daily that Easy gained as many enemies as he did loyal customers.

Easy was making money hand over fist. Little did he know that the millions he made could be directly attributed to the CIA and DEA operatives who supplied DeSosa with unlimited amounts of cocaine. Easy was a boy from the hood—a squirrel trying to get a nut; DeSosa was fulfilling his agreement with the government and the Reagan administration. It all worked like a well-oiled machine.

Their business relationship soon evolved into a personal one. DeSosa often invited Easy to break bread with him and his family, and sometimes DeSosa even dropped by the Hardaway house for a social call.

Detective Moore had been watching Easy and DeSosa's relationship progress. He was waiting for the day he could shake DeSosa's hand and thank him for blowing off the head of the man who'd destroyed his daughter's life. He was furious with DeSosa for falling back on his word.

"You fucking lied to me! We had a deal!" Moore had screamed when he stormed into DeSosa's new club, Baile Caliente, gun in hand, badge in the other. He was a man possessed. He didn't get very far before he was hemmed up by DeSosa's henchmen.

"You're a fucking liar, DeSosa . . . after all I did for you! All of the times I saved your ass!" Moore strained against the stronghold he was placed in, his veins cording against his skin.

DeSosa was very calm; his smug demeanor infuri-ated the detective even more.

"Detective, I think you have your son-in-law all wrong. You should try to get to know him. He is a good, loyal kid," DeSosa said, blowing a smoke ring in Moore's direction. "As for what you've done for me? I don't think you would want me to tell your chief what I've done for you over the years. I'm sure you didn't claim those bags of cash on your taxes," DeSosa countered, following up.

Moore's frustration mounted. He had watched his daughter run off with a known drug dealer, get herself pregnant and then marry the bastard. He hadn't even seen or held his own grandchildren. DeSosa had promised he would take Easy out. But what had he done but empower the man by supplying him with endless amounts of product? Now Easy was not only rich, but impossibly powerful, which placed his daughter and grandchild in even greater danger.

Detective Moore cursed DeSosa out and vowed that this wouldn't be the last time DeSosa or Easy heard from him.

"I will get my daughter out of this lifestyle if it's the last thing that I fucking do! Even if it means bringing you to your knees too," Moore threatened.

DeSosa had laughed at the peon detective. He wielded no power compared to the people DeSosa was involved with.

Shortly after Detective Moore's tirade and threats, the local police suddenly became very interested in one Eric "Easy" Hardaway and his associates. In a task force led by Moore, the NYPD became dedicated to putting Easy and his counterparts out of the crack cocaine business.

The first time they attempted to arrest Easy, they didn't have enough evidence to keep him detained. Following that, prosecutors from New York approached Easy and tried to get him to become a government informant. Easy had scoffed at their offer. He had laughed uproariously and told them to kiss his ass and speak to his lawyer; he was no snitch, he'd told them.

Those fucks actually thought he would talk to them about where the loads of cocaine they saw hitting the streets was coming from. Easy immediately reported this run-in with the NYPD to DeSosa. Needless to say, the NYPD's operation was short-lived. The locals had unwittingly stumbled into CIA territory, jeopardizing Operation Easy In, but not for long.

When Grayson Stokes swept through the NYPD Brooklyn South Task Force Office, he left captains shuddering in his wake. Detective Moore was forced to turn in his badge and shield; he became known throughout the law enforcement community as the detective who'd made the biggest drug fuckup in New York's history. He went home that night, placed his personal weapon between his lips and blew off his head.

Corine heard the report of her father's suicide from the eleven o'clock news. She never realized that her father's quest to destroy her husband, and to get his baby girl back, was ultimately the cause of his own demise.

Easy comforted Corine for the days and weeks that followed her father's suicide. Easy had held her, telling her it would be all right and that it was not her fault. But something about Moore's death had unsettled Easy. He'd known the man to be a very proud and religious person; he was a man who would never have taken his own life.

Easy consulted Rock about his need to investigate Moore's death. From a clean-cut ex-Marine, to an ex-CIA cleaner, to a drug kingpin hit man, Rock had no clue what he'd stepped into, until it was too late. All he wanted to do was live a quiet, circumspect life. But he also felt very loyal to Easy and would do anything to help his friend; loyalty was a trait ingrained in Rock's DNA.

Rock immediately set out to discover as much information as possible about the circumstances surrounding Moore's suicide. Rock briefed Easy in person about the information he came across. Only once had they spoken over the phone about the information Rock had learned about the CIA's involvement with DeSosa.

Rock regretted this slipup until the day he died.

The CIA had been tapping all of Easy's phones. Rock's revelation about the CIA's plans to distribute crack cocaine in poor neighborhoods had raised red flags.

Rock, of course, had tried talking Easy out of the game. Unwittingly, Easy had been a pawn of the government, helping to kill off his own people. Rock thought the decision would be a no-brainer.

Easy had been very unsettled with the information Rock had provided him with, but there was no easy and quick way out. To Rock's great dismay, he continued with the farce. After all, they both were aware that the only quick and sure way out of the game was through death. Neither was prepared for that inevitability. Nevertheless, Rock vowed to protect Easy, no matter what.

Naturally, Grayson Stokes was not pleased to hear that Rock Barton, one of his debriefed cleaners, was smack-dab in the middle of Operation Easy In. Rock

served as the catalyst for the CIA's decision to turn Rolando DeSosa against Easy Hardaway. They needed
a scapegoat for the mayhem that would ensue when
DeSosa turned against his protégé.

Stokes set about planting seeds of doubt in DeSosa's
head about Hardaway's allegiance to him. When
Stokes presented DeSosa with pictures that he'd taken
of the NYPD hauling Easy into the precinct, DeSosa
quickly wrote Easy off as a traitor. Stokes convinced
DeSosa that Easy had turned government informant.

Easy's latest discussions with DeSosa about leaving
the game was the final nail in his coffin. Easy Hardaway had reneged on his deal, and for that he must be
eliminated.

DeSosa sentenced Hardaway to the worst sort of
death—death by the hands of his oldest son, his name-
sake Eric Junior. Where DeSosa was from, a man
killed by his own offspring let people know he was the
lowest of the low, the scum of the earth. In DeSosa's
mind traitors like Easy were deserving of such a fate.

Chapter 12

Sins of a Father

Rolando DeSosa slammed his fists down on his desk until the sides of his hands went numb. He made an animalistic moaning sound, like he'd been mortally wounded. Pain was etched in every worry line on his face. His rage was palpable, and everybody in the room felt like it was alive—a big ugly monster standing in the middle of the room.

Arellio stood up to remove the pictures from his father's desk. He was kicking himself now for giving them to his father, but he didn't know what else to do, whom he should turn to. He reached out to grab the photos, but DeSosa came down on his hand, hard. He gave Arellio a look that would have felled a small creature. Arellio snatched his hand back and sighed. He thought it morbid that his ailing father wanted to stare at the disfigured and depraved photographs of his brother.

"*Papi*, let me take them away," Arellio whispered, trying to reach out to his father. "We will get whoever is responsible for this," Arellio consoled, stepping around the desk and clapping his hand on his father's shoulder.

DeSosa let his head hang low. Arellio could hear a cry bubbling up from deep inside his father's chest. He had never seen his father so broken down; it was killing him to see his father in this condition.

Rolando DeSosa hadn't cried since he was a boy in the Dominican Republic and his mother had been shot during an uprising in the small, poor ghetto where he had grown up. He'd cried for what seemed like an eternity over his mother's dead body inside their make-shift tin-roofed home. For seven days he stood by her decomposing body, along with his little brother, and prayed for a miracle that would bring his mother back to life.

DeSosa had become hardened by the event and had never shed tears for anybody since. But today the tears came and they could not be stopped. He wailed for his second-born child. Family meant the world to DeSosa. Someone would pay for his son's death. Revenge was high on DeSosa's list of rules to live by. If people went around committing evils without any consequences for their actions, the world would be an inhospitable place for everyone.

"It had to be Junior," Arellio said, breaking the silence, squeezing his father's shoulder in commiseration. "He was the only person . . . the only one who you recently had a problem with. We have to find him and fuckin' destroy him." He hoped that by steering his father toward avenging his brother's untimely death, he could bring him out of his melancholy state.

"No," DeSosa whispered, his voice cracking like a woman's.

Arellio stepped from behind his father and looked at him oddly. "*Papi*, don't tell me no. You can't protect these fuckin' bastards. I know Junior was the one who did this shit. . . . There's nobody else. . . ." Arellio was decisively protesting his father's dismissal; his eyes were ablaze with rage.

"No!" DeSosa snapped once more; his aching hands were clenched tightly in front of him. The veins in his neck pulsed dangerously close to the surface.

Arellio visibly shuddered at his father's grating, high-pitched shout.

"I took care of Junior," DeSosa whispered regretfully. "But it wasn't him. I knew it wasn't him. I thought he was lying to me, so I put Phil on him. Junior is taken care of, but this—this was not his doing. He didn't have the heart or the balls," DeSosa was saying, shaking his head as if he had all the regrets in the world sitting on his shoulders.

Arellio fell back onto an empty chair like the wind had been knocked out of him. "But who else could it have been? Who would do that to him, *Papi*?" Arellio asked. He could not fathom who would commit such a heinous act on his brother, who everyone knew was harmless, soft even.

"It was somebody who knew him, *Papi*. Whoever it was, they followed him," Arellio started, his voice cracking. He could not believe his poor, unsuspecting younger brother had gotten caught out there like that. The story would be all over the news. Their family would be humiliated.

DeSosa was rocking now; it was a habit he'd picked up since he'd been confined to a wheelchair. He heard his son rambling on about the possible suspects, but DeSosa wasn't really listening. There was one possible suspect that neither of them had discussed.

"It is her," DeSosa admitted in an almost inaudible whisper. "She came back for us, once and for all. She was here. . . . I can feel it," he wailed, inhaling a shaky breath.

One of his men had reported that the nanny had been spotted snooping around in his office. DeSosa had waved it off. He had met the nanny and believed her to be a harmless presence in his home. But now he saw the nanny in a new light—as a skillful, crafty and dangerous individual. She had infiltrated his home under false pretenses. She'd been right under his nose the entire time, laughing at them and plotting their downfall. "Who, *Papi*? What are you talking about? You're talking crazy. . . . You think a woman killed Guillermo?" Arellio asked in rapid succession. In his mind there was no way a woman could have inflicted that degree of damage on his brother. "*Papi* . . . answer me. What are you talking about?" he pressed.

DeSosa couldn't even look at his son. His father never hung his head for anything; he had too much pride for that. Arellio could feel his blood pressure rising with every minute that passed. He wanted to shake the answers out of his father, but he knew his emotional and physical state was already on very shaky ground.

"*Papi*, what did you do? What do you know?" Arellio raised his voice and placed both of his hands flat on the front of DeSosa's desk.

DeSosa could hear his son's labored breaths exit his flaring nostrils. He had no choice but to come clean and tell Arellio everything.

"Everybody out!" DeSosa came to life with renewed vigor. All of his men looked at him strangely. He hadn't been left without bodyguards in years, even when he visited with his own children. "I said get the fuck out! Everybody out!" he barked again, a feral look in his eyes. "I need to speak with my son," DeSosa whispered. His voice went high, then lowered like a wave at high tide.

His bodyguards and other workers filed out of the room.

"Sit down, Arellio," DeSosa said gravely, nodding toward the chair.

Arellio's chest felt heavy with dread as he sat on the chair.

"I have to tell you everything. It may mean the difference between your life and your death. I've already lost one son because of my sins. I don't want to lose you as well," DeSosa revealed. That was the closest DeSosa had ever come to saying "I love you" to his son. DeSosa closed his eyes and started at the beginning. Confession was good for the soul, or so they said. He needed to prepare his son for what was surely to come. He needed to give him as much information about the lady assassin as he had. The more he knew, the better chance he had of coming out alive in the end.

New York, 2006

Grayson Stokes dropped the envelope on DeSosa's lap. He was flustered that his word wasn't enough.

"I guess I have to make you a believer, huh, DeSosa?" Stokes chuckled while he waited for DeSosa to spill out the contents.

DeSosa jutted his jaw. He didn't care for Stokes. In fact, he hated the ground Stokes walked on. But DeSosa realized that Stokes and the CIA owned him now. It was either get down or lay down, when it came to the government spooks. DeSosa shook out the contents of the package. It only took him a few seconds to realize what he was looking at. His eyebrows shot up involuntarily at the sight. It was too late to try to put on a poker face; Stokes had already taken notice of his reaction.

"Now do you believe it?" Stokes asked, watching DeSosa's breathing pick up speed. "I don't have to lie to you . . . ever," Stokes said triumphantly, smirking.

DeSosa shuffled the pictures; he studied each one separately, hoping his eyes were deceiving him. His hopes were dashed. DeSosa's eyes bugged out when he examined a close-up photo of Easy, standing with his hands shoved into his pockets and talking to two detectives. The next shot was of Easy looking around suspiciously, like he was afraid he was being watched. All of these poses were the signs of a police informant. The sight sent a wave of stabbing cramps through DeSosa's lower abdomen.

Maricon, cabron! DeSosa screamed in his head. He positioned his lips into a straight line and rolled his eyes. He looked up at Stokes. "I would have never believed it. He was always loyal . . . so driven," DeSosa said disappointedly, trying very hard to keep a straight face. He didn't want Stokes to see how betrayed he felt.

"Well, DeSosa, the old saying goes, 'There's no honor among thieves.' I guess there's no honor among drug kingpins either," Stokes posited, chortling.

"So what now?" DeSosa asked, although he already knew the answer. He wanted to find Easy Hardaway and personally cut his balls off. He hated being deceived, especially by one of his own men. To think that Easy was trying to set him up made DeSosa's fucking blood boil.

"I want you to have your men get his son . . . the son with all of the problems. Who is going to notice if one schizo kid acts a bit crazier?" Stokes asked matter-of-factly. He spoke as if he were asking DeSosa to pick up a loaf of bread from the store. The man was ruthless and cold-blooded, always looking to get a man in his Achilles' heel.

"A couple of days of this stuff, and we'll have Hardaway's kid working for us," Stokes stated confidently. He pushed a small metal case toward DeSosa nonchalantly, like he was offering him a drink.

DeSosa looked down at the silver case and then back up at Stokes. This bastard is crazy! *His face must've betrayed his thoughts because Stokes started laughing.*

"Open it," *Stokes urged him, smiling like a Cheshire cat. DeSosa did as he was asked. Inside were five small unlabeled bottles of liquid that resembled immunization shots. There were also five injection syringes in sealed packages. DeSosa raised one eyebrow. This was all too much.*

"This is what you'll give the boy, once you pick him up. It's what we like to call our truth serum, mind control. Trust me, he will work like a robot for us," *Stokes explained.*

DeSosa's face was drawn into a scowl as he glared at the sick piece of shit standing before him.

"Ah, Rolando, you're too nice. It won't kill him. Just makes him do what we say. And Easy and his wife . . . well, with the boy's behavior they won't know the difference. You know the boy already has a lot of mental issues," *Stokes continued, laying out his depraved plan.*

DeSosa was astonished that Stokes had already had this plan all mapped out. It sent a shudder down DeSosa's spine. If he didn't know any better, he would have thought that he was dealing with el diablo himself.

Stokes read doubt and hesitation in DeSosa's face, so he toughened up his stance.

"Do as you are told, Rolando, and we'll always be on the same page," *Stokes threatened vaguely. With a grave snap of his fingers, he and his men were gone.*

DeSosa lost sleep over the task at hand. However, when he looked at the faces of his own sons and thought about his line of work, he decided that he had no choice. It was do or die.

DeSosa wasted no time carrying out the dastardly deed of his puppet master. His men coaxed Eric Junior off the streets as he left his session with his psychiatrist. It was much like the way DeSosa had coaxed Easy into his trap in the beginning—using his reputation and his men to ask for an exclusive meeting. Eric Junior had been excited that his father's boss, the only man ranked higher than Easy, had asked to see him.

Eric Junior had been stable on his medication for a few months when DeSosa asked to see him. Things had even been going well at home. His father had started grooming him for the business, showing him things about the streets and dropping little jewels of street knowledge on the boy. Though he still had the occasional outburst, they were on a much smaller scale than before he was diagnosed with psychosis.

When he was brought to DeSosa the first time, Eric Junior was smiling, all goofy and childlike. DeSosa took one look at the overzealous kid and didn't have the heart to fuck with his head—not yet, anyway. So he had the boy come back a few times, and told Eric Junior to keep it between them. He made it crystal clear that if Eric Junior told Easy about their meetings, it would jeopardize Eric Junior's chance at moving up without his father.

Eric Junior bought the story and kept the information from his father, but there was no way he could keep it from his brother. He wanted to make sure his brother knew he was no peon, and so he boasted to him one day about his meetings with DeSosa. His brother didn't pay him any mind, thinking that his medications were causing him to hallucinate.

DeSosa thought he could work on the boy's head, brainwash him without giving him any CIA poison, but the process was taking too long for Stokes. When

Stokes found out that he wasn't giving the boy the serum, he threatened DeSosa's family with bodily harm. That quickly put DeSosa back on track with the plan, with little room for deviation.

Eric Junior showed up for a meeting with DeSosa, hoping to talk to the kingpin about giving him his own slice of the business. He needed to get out from under his father's thumb and make a name for himself. As soon as he got to the front door, he was ambushed, knocked out, blindfolded and driven to a remote location.

When Eric Junior regained consciousness, he found himself on a gurney, tied down with restraints. He fought futilely against the ties. His face was etched with terror as he looked around at all of the frightening faces. He fought long and hard, but his body betrayed him and finally gave out.

The first injection of the drug had burned going in.

"Aggh! What the fuck!" he'd screamed. Eric Junior's body had bucked and seizured.

DeSosa thought the boy looked like a lab rat on the experiment table. The boy's eyes had bugged out of his head; his jaws started flexing involuntarily and veins all over his body were cording against his skin. Eric Junior's eyes were glazed over; his mouth hung slack and saliva dripped down his chin. The boy looked like he was going to convulse until he was dead.

DeSosa's men had been scared to death at his reaction to the drug. After all, it wasn't intended to kill him. They were all a bit relieved when the boy's body went limp.

Then the brainwashing session began. He was told his father was the enemy. He needed to kill Easy because his father was going to try to kill him, or, worse, would try to send him to live in a mental institution.

He was told that the only person he could trust was Rolando DeSosa.

The boy was dropped off a block away from his home. It had taken him hours to find his way home on that first day. He'd felt so disoriented and couldn't remember where he was going and why he was on the street.

DeSosa repeated the process five more times, as instructed by Stokes. The boy's mind deteriorated faster than Stokes had expected. Stokes was a happy camper. He'd even paid DeSosa a rare compliment.

"Maybe I should hire you as a CIA mind control expert," Stokes had joked.

DeSosa hadn't cracked a smile.

After what he'd done to Easy's son, DeSosa avoided Easy Hardaway like the plague. DeSosa also didn't trust that Easy wasn't trying to set him up; he was a police informant, after all.

Each time Easy asked for a meeting with DeSosa, the older man refused. Whenever Easy called, DeSosa was real short with him. Easy had always received his kilos directly from DeSosa, but suddenly there was a middleman.

DeSosa's sketchy behavior did nothing for Easy's already growing suspicions about DeSosa. With Rock buzzing in his ear, Easy started to see things differently. He'd been stressed beyond the norm. His home life had grown chaotic.

Eric Junior had begun acting erratically again. Easy had been trying to reel Eric Junior in, but the boy had other ideas. He wanted his own business, to do things his own way. This posed a major problem for Easy. Had he been one of Easy's other workers, he might've found himself going ghost a long time ago, but this was his son.

Then there was Easy's worker Junior, who had been giving Easy a lot of push-back and resistance lately. Junior was still mad that Easy had commissioned Rock to make Junior's best friend disappear. The man had been a liability from day one, but it was hard to convince Junior to see it from his perspective.

The reality of Easy's world had caught up with him—the distrust, the danger, the family matters— and he simply wanted out. He'd stacked some paper and was ready to quit the game. There were just too many dangers, too many signs to ignore. He needed to cut his losses and move on. He realized it wasn't going to be that simple, and so he'd requested a meeting with DeSosa to tell him face-to-face that he was leaving the game once and for all.

DeSosa again refused to meet with Easy. That was all the confirmation Easy needed. Rock was right; Easy needed to get out of the game.

"Rolando . . . it's Easy. Nah, I asked for a meeting and you refused. I'm letting you know I'm out. I'm done," Easy had announced, his voice wavering, just like his emotions.

Rock had sat stock-still as Easy made his announcement. He realized that the decision would come with consequences. When Easy hung up the line, Rock could see the trepidation on his face. Rock was struck with a bout of chest pains. What had he done?

"Yo, Rock, something about this just doesn't feel right, man. DeSosa was way too calm," Easy said, falling back on his chair.

Rock was quiet as he contemplated this.

Just then, Easy's phone rang again. He looked at the number displayed on the small screen and sighed. He pointed at the phone, signaling to Rock that the call wasn't good.

Easy inhaled, then exhaled loudly before picking up the line.

"Yeah," he answered.

"There is nothing you can do or say to change my mind. I'm gettin' outta the game. I'm an old man now. I've grown out of all of this shit," Easy lied. The truth was, he didn't trust DeSosa one bit—not after all that had transpired with his wife and his son.

"C'mon, DeSosa . . . ain't no reason to raise your voice. I should be the one pissed with you. I hear you been talkin' to my son. He is not going to go against me," Easy assured the man.

DeSosa stumbled over his words. He couldn't believe Easy knew that he'd been speaking to Eric Junior.

"You can make all of the threats you want. I'm out of the game," Easy said with finality before he disconnected the line.

That call had sealed his fate in more ways than one. Easy knew there would be consequences for his action; he just hoped he'd be able to live through them.

Arellio DeSosa was hanging on his father's every word. He knew his father was ruthless, but using a man's son to do his dirty work seemed beneath the DeSosa name.

"So you killed him?" Arellio asked. He knew the story of Easy Hardaway's death and the massacre of his entire family. He never knew his father was involved in it.

DeSosa nodded. "I sent them back with the boy. Easy suffered at the hands of his own son," DeSosa whispered.

Arellio still looked at him, confused. His father had gone over the entire long story, but still there was no mention of a girl. DeSosa could read the questions in his son's eyes.

"There was one girl left alive. When Stokes gave us the green light, he told us the whole family was home. He lied. He knew the girl would run to Barton. He knew Barton would train her. He had altered Barton's mind, like a robot. Stokes allowed Barton to train the girl to be an assassin so he could get rid of me when the time came. So he could bury his secrets—the government's secrets—with me and my entire family," DeSosa revealed.

"So he was the one who led her right to us," Arellio replied, like the pieces of the puzzle were finally coming together.

His father nodded his agreement. "She was here," DeSosa announced.

Arellio's eyebrows shot up. "The fucking nanny!" Arellio belted out, scrambling up from his chair and snatching the door open with a fury.

"Cyndi! Cyndi!" he screamed, his panicked voice echoing throughout the house.

The sun was shining down on the quiet neighborhood. The sounds of kids going off to school and fathers, with legitimate jobs, kissing their wives before heading off to work had already ceased. This was the time of day no one would be expecting anything. It was also the time of day that the DeSosas were beginning to stir, crawling awake after their previous night of criminal activities.

Candice knew all of their schedules by heart. She knew what time the eldest son went to confer with the father; what time Cyndi went to the nail salon; even what time DeSosa was given a sponge bath. But today would be different; today they would be grieving together and coming up with a strategy to avenge Guillermo's death.

How dare someone fuck with a DeSosa, right? Candice scoffed at their bullshit family pride. *How dare someone fuck with the Hardaways is more like it.*

She watched and waited for the right time to strike.

Crouching down, with her back rounded, she rested her elbows on her knees; her feet were planted flat so she could steady herself. *Crouching Tiger, Hidden Dragon,* she thought with a smirk. Her legs were spread, and her feet were lined up with each hip, just like Uncle Rock had taught her. *A sound base that can absorb gunshot recoil.*

She placed her dominant eye into the space on the round scope connected to the AR-15 and closed the other eye. Things came into focus real fast. Her ears filled with the rushing sound of her own labored breaths. Huge eagle-sized butterflies banged around inside her stomach now. She felt a sickening rush of anxious energy that made her feel powerful.

She spotted movement in the scope and adjusted it to focus in on her target. The eye of the scope was so precise and powerful; it was like the target was standing right in front of her. *Bam. Never know what hit you.*

There would be no more fucking target practice for Candice. No more getting beat to the punch. No more punking out or getting too emotional to stay on task. Nothing else mattered to her anymore.

Keeping her body as stiff and still as she could, Candice moved the pad of her trigger finger. She tested herself to see how steady she could be. A fine bead of sweat cleared a path down the side of her face. It tickled as it ran over the edge of her mouth and sneaked into her partially parted lips. Candice tasted the salt of her own sweat; it was a sign of things to come.

The anticipation inside her had built to a crescendo. She wanted to scream, to let out some of the tension. She blew out a cleansing breath, instead. There were only a few more targets left and she'd be done. Justice would be served for her family and for Uncle Rock, and she would finally have the peace she craved in her life. *Trigger. Trigger. Trigger,* she chanted in her head. Another thing she'd been taught by Uncle Rock. He'd taught her that repeating the word would keep her mind off her trigger pull and keep her from anticipating the shot. All she had to do was watch and wait for the perfect shot—a clean shot to the head. Maybe she'd get 'em between the eyes, but she would settle for a nice five-ring chest shot, if she absolutely had to.

Her legs were starting to burn as the newly formed sweat beads dripped into her eye; still, she didn't dare to move. Her arms trembled from the position she was in, but she kept her poise. This was her last chance, and she felt like she needed to take the opportunity before she lost it. Suddenly her heart jerked.

Right now. Clear shot. No hesitation. Focus. Trigger. Trigger. Trigger.

The target had been on the move a few minutes before but now stood still. There was nothing in her way.

Trigger. Trigger. Trigger. Now! Candice screamed inside her head. Her body tensed, but her hands did what they had been trained to do.

Candice was surprised by the sound of the click; the slack was out of the trigger. The trigger was all the way back one second and clicking to return to position the next second.

Again. Again. Until the threat is eliminated. Candice's head swirled with instruction. *One more time. Trigger. Trigger. Trigger.*

The sound of crashing glass brought things into focus for Candice now. It was done. Then the silent air was split in half by the shrill screams of a female voice. *Confirmation.* Instinctively, her shoulders slumped and she let out a long sigh. The hard part was over.

Loud screams and the eruption of pandemonium brought her back to reality. She wasn't at the range practicing with Uncle Rock's AR-15 anymore. Her muscles ached with tension and she was burning hot from the sun beating down on her in the hours spent lying in wait.

Panic struck her like a 1,000-pound boulder. She had to get away from here. Her breath came out in short, sharp pants. Candice's hands shook as she unhooked the legs from the weapon and folded them down. Then she handled the weapon like it was a crown jewel. She placed it in the case Uncle Rock had made especially for it and then slung the leather strap of the case around her chest and let it hang down her back. She was on the move within seconds.

Sirens could be heard in the distance now. This wasn't like the last time. . . . There would be no delayed reactions from the police and ambulances. Candice knew that hitting the victim in the home was risky business. There would be many more potential witnesses, for instance. But she'd practiced so many times, and she felt there was little room for error on her part. She employed every rule and tool Uncle Rock had provided her with to execute the job with expert precision. Candice thought Uncle Rock would probably give her an A+ on her work today. She'd even snagged a pair of black leather gloves and worn them. She was almost as good as he was, a professional cleaner. That made her smile.

With the confidence of an Olympic triathlete, she moved her body with great agility and speed. "Twenty seconds after kill shot. Damn, Candy, you are good," she complimented herself softly.

This time she didn't worry about who might be watching her. She wanted them to know she was coming for them too. If Candy got any harder, she would turn into cement.

Chapter 13

A Battle with Darkness

Dana Carlisle raised her arms above her head and arched her back. "Mmm," she moaned, then let her arms flop down at her sides. A huge yawn followed her feline-like stretch. Boredom was the order of the night. There was nothing on television that she hadn't already seen or was even remotely interested in watching.

Blowing out an exasperated breath, she got up from the couch and padded over to the window of the cabin. She clipped her fingers through the espresso-colored faux wood blinds and peeked out the window. Darkness. She called it her security sweep for the night.

When she first arrived at the cabin, she performed full gun-in-hand security sweeps of the entire house and area around it. Now she just made sure she sat tight and waited to be rescued. Something about the peace of the darkness actually made her feel whole and comforted. The sound of footsteps behind her startled her out of her reverie. It could only be one of three people, anyway. Carlisle wished that person had just stayed her ass in bed. Slowly she turned to see who was intruding on her alone time.

Carlisle's mood blackened at the sight of Elaina on the staircase. She rolled her eyes and turned her back to the window, hoping the darkness would wrap its arms around her to make her blend into the night. She really didn't feel like playing houseguest with Elaina right now.

Elaina shuffled her feet and moved into the kitchen. Carlisle was sure she had been seen; yet no words were exchanged. Carlisle was used to Elaina's cold, silent treatment. Lucky for her, the kids loved her and she was able to spend the daytime playing board games and singing along with the karaoke machine.

Carlisle didn't care too much for Elaina's prissy attitude. She was pretty fucking ungrateful, seeing that Carlisle had picked up and agreed to protect Elaina's unfaithful ass. Frankly, the only reason Carlisle had agreed to come out to Deep Creek Lake and stand guard over Tucker's family was because of her deep feelings for him and concern for the well-being of his children. Either way, Carlisle didn't like Elaina; she prayed that when all of the danger had subsided, Tucker would drop the bitch like a hot potato.

Carlisle could hear Elaina fussing around with the teakettle and rummaging through the cabinets. For the most part they avoided each other whenever possible. They were like polar opposites, circling around one another. Both were hyperaware of the other, but neither made the effort to initiate any kind of personal relationship.

There were so many days that Carlisle had been tempted to break the wall of silence that had settled between the two women—to tell her exactly what was going on. Or maybe talk about Tucker as a family man and as a professional. However, Elaina's stony demeanor kept her at a very formal distance.

Carlisle walked back over to the little end table next to the patchwork, paisley-decorated couch and picked up her pack of cigarettes. She examined the pack. Only three more left. Shit! She'd have to go into town tomorrow. Smoking was a habit she'd reacquired in the past few weeks. She had quit back in college; but fucking around with Tucker and his government conspiracy games, Carlisle needed something stronger than caffeine to calm her nerves.

She stepped outside to light a smoke, and the cold, bitter air hit her arms. She cursed to herself when she realized her jacket hung over the back of one of the dinette chairs in the kitchen, where Elaina was playing house. Carlisle let out a long sigh. It was either go into the lion's den to get her jacket or stand out on the blustery porch and smoke in peace. A little cold never killed anyone, right?

The crisp night air blowing off the lake immediately whipped around her face and slapped at her bare arms. Springtime up at the lake didn't feel quite as nice as it sounded. Carlisle lit her cigarette and stepped down the three steps of the cabin porch. She took a toke and shivered. Aside from the small porch light, there was nothing but blackness in front of her.

Good thing she never left without her Glock. A few more drags off the cigarette and she felt like it wasn't even worth it anymore. She dropped her cigarette and mashed the lit end out with her sneaker tip. Her nerves were settled, but her teeth were chattering.

Turning around swiftly, Carlisle took the three steps in one long stretch of her legs. Just as she passed the two Adirondack chairs on the porch, a sound startled her. Carlisle whipped her head to the left, toward the noise. It must be that raccoon again trying to rummage through their trash. She still went to her gun; it could also be a damn big-ass papa black bear. She listened again for the sound and heard a strange knocking noise. Carlisle crumpled her face, part aggravation, part confusion.

With a two-handed grip on her gun, she moved toward the noise. This time the sound came from her right. Something wasn't right. Squinting her eyes against the dark, Carlisle lifted her gun and extended it out in front of her.

"Who's out there?" she called out. There was no answer.

She moved from the other side of the porch now. Fuck it. Carlisle was going to go inside, bolt down the door and hunker down like Tucker had told her to do. Just as she reached for the doorknob, she heard the loud screams of the teakettle inside the house. She jumped, nearly peeing on herself.

Fuck Elaina and her gotdamn late-night tea sessions.

Carlisle grabbed hold of the doorknob, ready to cuss Elaina out, when she saw something out of her peripheral vision. A scream lodged in the back of her throat as the shadowy figure placed a gloved hand over her nose and mouth and kicked her legs from under her. Her gun dropped with a clang. Her body went limp.

Unfortunately, with the teakettle whistling loudly on the stove, Elaina never heard the commotion. Nor did she hear the stranger's footsteps enter the cabin.

Tuck sat outside of the Monte Carlo, drumming his fingers on his steering wheel. He checked his watch again and let out a long sigh. Candice had told him to meet her there, but she was nowhere to be found. He'd gone inside and asked for every name he could think of—Candice Hardaway (she wouldn't be stupid enough to use that name he'd thought, but anything was possible), Candy Barton (better possibility) or Shana Bellamy (maybe she would pay homage to her dead friend). None of the names were listed in the Monte

Carlo's guest information system. Tuck went back out to his car and waited.

Candy had to know he would come. They'd shared a night together; they had a deep connection, or so he thought. In his mind's eye he could still see the silhouette of her flat stomach, round hips and athletic legs. He remembered the tightness of her holding him captive; the possessiveness he had felt toward her when he realized no other man had touched her in such a way.

Suddenly Tuck shuddered as he thought about that night. It had been a mistake. He realized that now. He was an adult—a married man, the father of two children. Candy had been an eighteen-year-old virgin girl on a revenge mission. He had been seduced by her brains and body, but there was no real basis to their relationship. Candy was a fleeting fancy; his wife, on the other hand, was the real deal.

Tuck looked at his watch again and swore that if she didn't show up soon, he would leave. She had already stood him up yesterday, but today he felt like he'd be able to catch her unaware. So like a crackhead who needed one last hit, he waited.

Tuck practiced what he would say to her when she arrived. "I don't want anything from you. I don't even want to try to stop you from killing your enemies. I just want to give you these." That's what he'd say; then he'd hand over Easy's files for her safekeeping.

Tuck knew that getting Candice to trust him was a long shot, but he would still make the effort. Regardless of a one-night stand or not, Candice had serious trust issues. He told himself he was there for one thing, and one thing only: to give her the files so she would have insight into her father's life. He owed her that much at least.

But that wasn't entirely the whole truth, though. Candy did have good reason to suspect Tuck of ulterior motives.

At the end of his meeting with Stokes, Tuck had promised to hand Candy over to him to ensure the safety of his family and himself. He'd convinced Stokes that sending in a tail or setting a trap wouldn't work with someone like Candy.

"Trust me. Let me get her on my side and then I'll bring her right to you," Tuck had assured.

Being in the business of subterfuge, Stokes was highly skeptical of Tucker's plan. Tucker reminded him that if they knew where Candy was all along, they could have easily picked her up a long time ago. But the problem was that Candy could change colors quicker than a chameleon.

"Remember, you thought you were God . . . but Rock Barton and Candy Hardaway might be the bane of your existence. She trusts me already," Tuck had argued.

Stokes had finally given in to his demands. He had few options to begin with.

"She trusts you, Agent Tucker . . . but can I trust you?" Stokes asked doubtfully.

Tucker never answered his question. Instead, he took the additional Hardaway files and exited the room. It was all a guessing game, anyway; no one really knew the other's intentions.

But actions always spoke louder than words.

Candice silently watched Tuck from a distance. What was she even doing here?

Tuck had promised her information about her father, but he could have also been setting her up. Her heart was at war with her mind. She didn't really trust anyone from her past. The only people whom she trusted implicitly were dead.

Lately she could not stop thinking about that night. She could almost feel the same hot rush that had suffused her body when she had accepted him into her mouth, their tongues intertwining in a sensual dance.

Candice had kissed Tuck like her life depended on it. She felt a throbbing pulse between her legs, much like she had during her first time, with Tuck. It was a feeling so intense that she would've done anything to feel it again.

Candice closed her eyes for a split second, picturing him as he moved his hot mouth from her lips and licked his way down her neck and then to her breasts. She had shuddered, needle pricks all over her body, when Tuck had licked her areola until she lost her breath.

Tuck had grabbed his manhood and placed it gently against Candice's moist flesh. When he bore down into her softness, Candice had felt a flash of fire between her legs, which had quickly turned into an all-out explosion of pain. She opened her mouth now, the same as she had done that night. Her body was experiencing the sensations all over again. Candice hadn't stopped him from taking her virginity that night. And now she couldn't stop thinking about it.

Candice wanted to slap herself when she realized she had let her mind drift to the past. Shaking her head from left to right, she rubbed her arms roughly and shook off those distracting thoughts.

The first day Tuck had come to the Monte Carlo, Candice watched him, amused at his bewilderment. Did he really think she would be dumb enough to meet up with him in such a public place? She watched Tuck get frustrated at being stood up, getting in and out of his car repeatedly with the look of defeat on his face. When he left, Candice watched closely for any tails or any sign that he had brought his crooked law enforcement friends with him. To her surprise, Candice had not noticed anyone following or watching him. No red taillights, no ghosts on foot and no other people materializing from the surrounding buildings when he'd left.

Still not convinced of his claims of innocence, Candice decided to watch Tuck for one more day. Shit, if he could be undercover for so long, pretending to be a common street dude, there was no telling what type of stunt he was capable of pulling off. Candice figured there was no such thing as being too careful. So she watched for a second day. And again there was no one mysteriously buzzing around. He hadn't met with anyone; he hadn't spoken to anybody on the street.

Perhaps Tuck was on the up-and-up, Candice concluded. Seeing him again that day, at the DeSosa home, had flustered her so much that it had almost taken her out of her game. She wanted to be sure she could handle things emotionally before she showed herself to him again.

When Tuck's car gurgled to life, she rushed from her hiding spot across the street from the Monte Carlo. She couldn't be sure he'd come back for a third day looking like a desperate asshole waiting for her. He didn't even see her coming.

The taps on the window nearly gave Tuck a heart attack. He jumped so hard that he hit his bald head on the roof of his car.

"Gotdamn!" he cried out, placing his hand over his chest in a clutch-the-pearls manner.

Candice ran around the front of the car and Tuck popped the door locks. Candice bustled into the passenger seat and hurriedly slammed the door. She shivered. Her nerves were screaming.

"You scared the shit out of me, Candy," Tuck gasped. He was still struggling to find his breath.

She wasn't the only one with hair trigger nerves. The fact that he seemed jumpy too made her feel superior in a silly, childish kind of way.

"Big, bad DEA agent scared of little ol' me." She chuckled sarcastically. Then her face got serious, and her lips twisted to the side. Tuck gave her a look that said *touché*. She'd scored a point for that one.

"Now, Agent Tuck, or whatever your name is, why do you want to see me so badly?" she asked. The undertone of her question was one part sassy, one part curious.

"Look, Candy, there are a lot of people looking for you right now. I am trying—"

"I don't give a fuck who is looking for me! I am looking for them too!" Candice boomed defensively, clipping off his conversation.

"Whoa, whoa . . . I'm here to help you, Candy. Everybody in the world is *not* out to hurt you."

Candy's vehemence had caught him completely off guard.

"Oh yeah? Says who? You? A fuckin' DEA agent who lies for a living? What the fuck do you know about who is trying to hurt me? Did you lose your entire family at the hands of these motherfuckers for absolutely nothing? Because they wanted to play government war games with the lives of innocent kids?" Candy screamed.

The incredible hurt was evident behind her words. Tuck was dumbfounded.

"I'm sorry about your loss, Candy. Trust me, this is not easy for me either. I know all about being betrayed by the government . . . and I was very fuckin' loyal to them. But I need to let you know there are people after you. You should've listened to Barton and gotten far away from here. Forget avenging your family's deaths. Getting away with your life is much more important," he retorted in all honesty.

"This was a mistake," she said, starting for the door handle. Her Glock dug into her side as she turned to make her escape.

"Wait!" he grabbed her arm.

"Don't ever put your hands on me again!" she shot back; her gun was in her hand just as quickly.

Tuck snatched his hand back like he'd just been stung by a bee. They were back to square one.

"Candy, I just want to help you. I swear. I put my entire family in danger just to help you. Let me," he pleaded.

Something about the pleading in his voice made her insides hot. Candice was angry with herself; she felt tears burning at the backs of her eyes. She was too fucking emotional these days.

"What did you really call me here for?" she asked, her voice cracking.

"I wanted to give you these," Tuck told her, reaching behind him into his backseat. He pulled up a thick packet. She furrowed her forehead at the stack of papers.

"Everything you need to know is right in here. Candy, your father was in a lot of shit. I want to warn you, some of this shit is very deep. Deeper than anything Barton could've even imagined," Tuck said in a foreboding tone.

Candice accepted the package, but she hesitated to look inside. She didn't want to learn anything about her father that would change her last view of him. In her eyes he was, and always would be, a stand-up family man who commanded respect and loved her more than anything in the world.

"Where did you get this, if you weren't working with them?" Candice asked, squinting her eyes.

"Let's just say I have friends in high places," Tuck replied.

"Yeah, that's just what I was afraid of. Thanks," she said in a low whisper.

Tuck nodded.

Before she left the car, Candice gave Tuck her cell phone number, though she didn't plan on having it for much longer. She knew all about the government's GPS tracking technology.

Tuck watched her disappear into the night. Now all he needed to do was get in touch with Carlisle and get his family the fuck out of Dodge.

Candice opened the notebooks as soon as she was alone. The curiosity was burning her up inside. She would read through her father's stories, but she wouldn't let it change her mind about what she had to do. There was still one more mission to carry out before she went ghost, once and for all.

"*My Life,*" she read aloud, already captivated.

Hardaway Household, 2006

Easy walked into his bedroom and found his wife sitting on the side of the bed. She had obviously heard him arguing on the telephone. The vibe in the entire house was tense, to say the least. Easy glanced at Corine and knew that this conversation would not go over well.

Corine sat stiffly upright, her body language completely closed off to him. Deep worry etched extra lines around her eyes and mouth; she seemed to have aged lately. When Corine wasn't angry with him, she was detached and aloof in her interactions with Easy. This shit was harder than he thought it could ever be. Getting out of the business was much harder than getting in.

"Corine, we need to talk," Easy told her. His voice was heavy with resignation.

She shuddered a little bit and looked down at her nails, anything to distract her mind. She knew they would be having this conversation sooner or later. Corine had expressed her dislike and distrust of the Dominicans on numerous occasions. Easy never listened to her; he always brushed off her concerns.

Easy sat down on his side of the bed; she stayed on her side; neither looked at the other.

"Listen, I want you to hear me out before you react crazy," Easy warned. He knew how hotheaded his wife could be at times.

She cleared her throat. Corine was ready for him; she had been preparing what she would say ever since she'd overheard his phone conversation with his regular confidant.

Easy continued talking. "We might have to leave Brooklyn, Corine. I think it's going to be best for us and for the kids to just take what we got and get far away from here. I'll find a new hustle," Easy announced gravely.

Her eyes went wide. She didn't even understand her shock. She should have felt relieved that he was getting out of the game. But uprooting the kids? Taking apart their lives? All of the sacrifices she'd made to build this life with him would be for nothing. Her insides grew hot.

"I told the Dominicans I wanted out. They ain't happy about this shit, Corine. It might mean war,"

Easy said, pinching the bridge of his nose. "I know I promised you that things would always be all right. I know you never wanted me to get down with them, but you have to trust me. I did all of this for us," he said, almost whispering.

It was always about Easy, never about Corine or the kids. He made all of the decisions—Corine and the kids were always an afterthought. His arrogance, even when trying to be humble, sent her over the top. Corine was on her feet like a demon had taken possession of her body and mind.

"I hate you! It was all for nothing! I hate you! You're a selfish piece of shit! I should have never married you, just like my daddy said!" she screamed.

Easy whirled around so fast—he almost gave himself whiplash. Her words hurt him deeper than a knife wound. Her reaction shook him to his core and totally caught him off guard. "Corine, I'm sorry." What else could he say to make up for the years of suffering she had experienced because of his poor life choices?

"You have no idea how you've ruined our lives! What about the sacrifices I've made? Huh? What about me—your wife? What real sacrifices have you made for this family, Eric? All you've ever cared about is making money!" Her caramel face turned almost burgundy with anger.

Easy worked his jaw. What the fuck was wrong with this woman? He could feel heat rising from his feet and climbing up. He put his hands out in a conciliatory fashion, trying to level with her.

"We've both made sacrifices, Corine. I have worked my ass off to give you this life. So you wouldn't have to work or do shit but sit around, shop and look fuckin' pretty!" Easy retorted.

The words hit her like a cold slap in the face. He immediately regretted the words after they'd left his lips. His wife's face crumpled and her eyes turned dark, like a storm was brewing inside. Corine doubled over at the waist, her body quaking with emotion.

"Yeah, all I ever did was fuck you, stay barefoot and pregnant, and spend your money, right, Eric? That's all I ever did for you, right? I should be kissing your feet with appreciation, huh? Fuck you, Easy Hardaway! You don't know what I've done for you—you have no fucking idea!" Corine erupted, propelled by her rage.

Easy was pissed now too. He was under enough stress without these dramatic outbursts from his wife.

"Did you ever think about me? How I walked away from my own family to be with you? How I lost myself to this lifestyle? What about my sacrifices!" Corine was screeching like a fishwife.

"Corine, I don't have time for this shit right now. I have shit to handle that you know nothing about," he grumbled.

Corine shoved an accusatory finger into his chest.

"Your little sacrifices don't mean shit in the scheme of things, Corine. And don't make your father into some kind of saint. He was a fuckin' crooked-ass cop who thought you were a prize to be won. Your mother always hated you, jealous of your relationship with your own father, so fuck your sacrifices. You don't even understand the meaning of the word," Easy boomed cruelly.

Corine had pushed him into a corner, and the only thing he could do was attack. In a knee-jerk reaction to his vituperative words, Corine reached out and slapped him across the face with all of her might.

She'd hit him so hard that the palm of her hand stung. Corine didn't know what had come over her, but it felt good to get her aggression out. She lifted her hand to slap him again, but her fingers curled involuntarily into a fist. She flew at him like an avenging angel.

"I hate you!" she growled, going wild on him.

Instinctively, Easy grabbed her wrists in defense. He held them tightly until he felt the tenseness leave her body.

"C'mon, we not gonna do this," he whispered. The last thing they needed to do was turn against one another.

Corine's knees suddenly buckled and she collapsed to the floor. She didn't have the fight in her anymore. She felt drained. She sobbed like a woman burying her dead baby.

Easy had no idea she would react to his news so violently. He got down on the floor with his wife, but she was beyond consoling.

"Corine, I'm sorry. It's going to be okay. I promise, just like from day one, I'm going to make it all okay," Easy lied. He didn't know how things would turn out. The truth was, he was scared to death for himself, for her and for their kids.

"No! It won't! They told me they wanted to get back at you! They said you were talking to the cops!" Corine wailed.

Easy's face folded into a frown. He looked at her like she'd lost her mind. What the hell was she talking about?

"Who? What? What are you talking about, Corine?" he asked incredulously.

"I didn't want to tell you! They wanted to hurt you. I didn't want to tell you," she rambled incoherently. Her voice was a shrill cacophony of pain. She rubbed her arms up and down, as if she had goose bumps.

"*Tell me what?*" Easy's voice boomed as he shook her shoulders. "*What are you talking about?*" he asked frantically.

"*They—they hurt me, Eric. They violated me. They wanted to get back at you. They took turns hurting me!*" Corine screeched, rolling around in pain.

The entire scene smacked of melodrama; Easy felt like he had been thrown into a bad soap opera. His ears began ringing. The room began to spin around him. He jumped up like his wife was a contagious disease. How could she have hidden something like this from him? She clearly didn't trust him enough to share the information with him.

"*Eric . . . please!*" she cried out, stretching out her hand for him. She knew this would be his reaction. She knew he wouldn't be able to handle it. "*Please!*" she begged again.

Easy began stalking the room like a caged animal overdue for a feeding.

"*When?*" he asked harshly. His eyes were closed in agony. He hadn't stopped moving.

She didn't answer.

"*When did it happen, gotdamn it?*" he boomed.

Corine jumped. Her body trembled with trepidation.

"*The day I had you pick me up from the hospital, when I told you someone had snatched my purse and made me fall. Remember my supposed mugging? My black eye and busted lip? I concocted that whole story. I didn't want you to find out the truth.*"

Easy furiously stalked over to the dresser and swiped everything onto the floor. He was panting and growling now. He felt like someone was choking the very air out of his body. He wanted to throw up. Corine cried out even louder.

"Tell me everything!" Easy barked. His palms were splayed flat on the emptied dresser top; his head was slung low between his shoulders.

"Don't make me, Eric. Please." She regretted that she'd ever gotten so emotional that she had broken her silence. She never wanted him to experience this sort of betrayal and hurt.

"Tell me now!" he barked, slamming his hands down on the dresser.

Corine closed her eyes and hugged herself. She opened her mouth and told Easy the whole truth. She recalled how she had left Macy's and had headed to her car, happy as a lark because she had just picked up two nice shirts for him. Corine loved nothing more than to surprise Easy with gifts, since he was always giving her beautiful tokens. When she got to her car, she placed her purse on top of the trunk and fished around in her pocketbook for her car keys.

While she was distracted with this task, a Hispanic man materialized out of nowhere. So did a van. She should've noticed when the van pulled too close to her car. When the man approached her, she felt a chill as his black eyes gazed at her a bit too long. A chill went up her spine. The man spoke in Spanish to her and appeared to be asking for her help. He was pointing to a car a few spots back.

Corine looked at him, confused. She couldn't understand anything he was saying. She was about to tell him she couldn't speak Spanish; but before she could get the words out, she felt a rush of wind behind her and felt a pointed pressure in her back.

She stumbled forward and the Hispanic man grabbed her. Another man had bum rushed her from behind. Within seconds, the two men, working together, had thrown her in that black van. She fought them off at first, scratching at skin, kicking, spitting and biting when she could.

All of her efforts were in vain. A black blindfold was securely tied over her eyes. She opened her mouth wide to scream and she smelled something strong. Not quite like alcohol, but more like hospital disinfectant. It burned her nostrils. Her brain felt blank and then her world went black.

When Corine regained consciousness, she cracked her eyes open but could only see little slivers of light through the blindfold. Her neck throbbed as she tried to move her head. She finally became aware of her entire body and the pain that permeated it. She moaned out loud. She felt a burning sensation between her legs and severe cramps in her abdomen. The pain was almost unbearable, but at least she wasn't dead. She tried again to lift her head, but she felt a pair of strong hands bearing down on her chest, forcing her back down.

Deep-voiced cackles sent chills down her aching spine. She squinted through the black material trying to make out shapes and faces, but it was nearly impossible. The shadows moved in front of her. This time she tried to move her arms, but they wouldn't budge; they had obviously tied them down. There was more Spanish being spoken. Foreign words filtered into her ringing ears. She felt hands on her legs. She jumped to kick the offending hands away, but they pulled her legs apart like a wishbone. She tried to scream, but the material from the gag cut into the corners of her mouth.

She might not be able to see them, but she could smell them clearly. A mixture of sweat, alcohol and hair grease assailed her nose. She wanted to vomit. She gagged but somehow managed to control her stomach. *If she didn't get a hold on herself, she would choke on her own vomit and die. And then her children would be without a mother, and her husband without a wife.*

She tried to scream as a man straddled her broken body. A hard slap to the face shut her up real quick. She knew one of them had gotten between her stretched legs. She prayed that God would watch over her children, for surely she would die today in the most humiliating fashion. Pain rocked through her abdomen like an earthquake as she felt him pounding into her body. Her vagina was raw with burning. She bit down into the gag as tears leaked from the corners of her eyes.

One after the other, they each took their turns with her. They performed sordid acts, violating her in the most sickening ways. After an eternity the violence on her body came to an end. By then, Corine had wrapped herself in a cocoon of disbelief and denial. Oddly enough, she thought of her father and how much she missed him.

In broken English a new voice cautioned, "Not too much'a bruises."

Why this man was saving her from bruises, when the men clearly planned to kill her, was beyond her understanding? The man called an end to their sick little party; for that, she was grateful. His voice was raspy, and his cologne smelled familiar, but she couldn't place the fragrance.

"Tell your husband what we did to you. Tell him, we know he is talking to the police and he'd better stop. Tell him, we said there's only one way out," the older gentleman had whispered, close to her face. She tried to turn her head toward him, but they pushed her face away.

Her attackers had been instructed to clean her up and drop her off back at her car.

When Corine was deposited back in the parking garage, she tried to make out their faces. But this time they were smart enough to wear disguises. Corine didn't know whether to start screaming for help or thank them for not killing her. Her head was all messed up.

When she put the key in the ignition, she didn't know what to do or where to go. Every car that drove by made her jump. She'd sat there for almost an hour, crying off and on. Her body ached so bad; she didn't think she could grip her steering wheel.

Corine wanted to call somebody, but they hadn't returned her pocketbook or her cell phone—she was given just a lone car key.

She couldn't ask for help from strangers. She didn't trust anyone right now. Worst of all, she didn't know how she could possibly tell Easy about what had happened to her during these last few hours. The news would devastate her husband, giving her attackers twice the satisfaction.

Corine decided she would take her lumps on this one. She would be strong and come up with a plausible story to explain the bruises that were already darkening her face. She needed to stick as close to the truth as possible—she would tell Easy she had been robbed. Yes! That would work. That would explain her black eye and busted lips. And her missing cell phone and purse.

Corine considered that Easy might not believe the story, since most of Brooklyn knew she was his wife and wouldn't dare fuck with her. She would simply have to stress to her husband that she believed her attack to be a random act of violence, as opposed to a calculated act.

She planned to put the trauma behind her and move forward with her life. She would hold her head up high and never let those bastards see her falling apart. Corine knew the risks she'd accepted when she agreed to become a hustler's wife. She knew that one day she would have to make the ultimate sacrifice; today, unfortunately, was that day.

Corine pulled her car over to the side of the road about five times before she arrived at the hospital. She stumbled into the emergency room and requested a female doctor. Corine was examined by the doctor. The doctor immediately ordered a rape kit and told Corine she'd have to wait for the results of the STD tests. That had unnerved Corine. She hadn't even considered the consequences of her rape. Aside from the STD, the men could have impregnated her as well. Her womb shuddered in revulsion. She snatched the Plan B pill from the doctor and swallowed it in a single gulp.

"Please . . . you can't tell my husband about this. You can't mention it around him," Corine pleaded, holding on tightly to the white lab coat.

The doctor looked at her like she had lost her mind.

"He won't ever look at me the same. I couldn't handle that on top of this," Corine half lied.

The doctor consented to her wishes, although very reluctantly. She recommended that if Corine was not going to share the truth with her husband that she at least join a support group for victims of rape. Corine agreed to give it careful consideration.

When Corine finally called Easy from the hospital, he sounded very close to near panic. He told her he had been worried sick about her and had about a hundred dudes scouring the streets looking for his wife.

Easy made it to Long Island College Hospital in record time. When he saw Corine's face, his anger *erupted like Mount Vesuvius. He seemed to buy the robbery story; for that, Corine was deeply relieved. Of course, he had about 50 million questions for her to answer, but his concern was mostly for her well-being as opposed to grilling her about her attack. He could get those details later, when she was able to think more objectively about the incident.*

Easy knew that a nigga in Brooklyn bold enough to touch his wife had to be on a suicide mission. Easy didn't waste any time. He went on a rampage. He was on the phone for hours at a time, trying to track down leads on who might have attacked his wife. Easy couldn't sleep or eat. He had to find the fuckers responsible for robbing his wife. He had his workers all over the streets, fanned out looking for a ghost. After a while the manhunt died down.

Easy remained calm but cautious. Corine was practically under house arrest for the next two months after the incident occurred. She had new locks put on the house, and a more enhanced security system installed. She was paranoid that the men who had hurt her would return. Corine fought through her nightmares and continued to put on a brave face in front of her husband and children.

Corine had secretly joined a rape crisis center support group, but that turned out to be too much of a challenge. Corine got tired of trying to get Easy to let her go out alone; she hated lying to him as well, so she eventually quit the center. Instead, she suffered in silence, not giving her victimizers the satisfaction of breaking her spirit.

Corine didn't know what had finally compelled her to tell Easy the truth about the events that had transpired so long ago. Perhaps he had pushed her too far by his selfish claims or by his dismissive attitude about the sacrifices she'd made for her family over the years. Nonetheless, Corine was relieved to have cleared the air between herself and Easy. Lately they had been growing apart, and a large part of the distance was a result of the dark secrets they had kept from each other.

Easy felt like he had been in a twelve-round boxing match by the time Corine finished reliving her ordeal. He felt like he was there when it all happened; she had relayed it in such detail. Listening to it, he was like a fly on the wall. Easy had collapsed on the floor with his wife and held her close to him, wishing he could squeeze all of the pain out of her. They had both cried together into the night.

Corine could not explain what had come over her, but the confession felt good for her soul, and good for their marriage. If they wanted to make their relationship work, they had to start trusting each other again.

The next morning Corine woke up and felt better than she had in a long time. She didn't want Eric's sympathy, just his love. She was going to keep it together for her family. What she had confessed would never leave the confines of their bedroom walls; Easy had promised her that much.

"Brianna's birthday party still needs to be planned," Corine announced in a rather husky tone. Her voice was still raw from all of the crying she had done the night before.

Easy gazed at his wife in true amazement; he could not believe that his wife was thinking about throwing a birthday party after all she had been through. She was truly a treasure above all treasures. He walked over to his wife and held her closely.

"I love you, baby. Have I told you that lately?" Eric said in a husky tone.

"No, you haven't, but I won't hold it against you. I'm done with holding grudges, especially against my own husband," Corine teased.

Eric rewarded her with a passionate kiss that nearly stole her breath away.

"Promise me that whatever you do to get revenge, you'll wait until after Brianna has her party. I know we may have to leave Brooklyn, but we need to make life as normal for our kids as possible," she said calmly.

Easy had been struck silent. He couldn't make that promise to his wife now.

"You know me so well, baby," Eric said. "I promise I won't do anything to ruin Brianna's party." That was the best he could offer her right now.

"I want this party to be huge," Corine said, too busy with party planning to pick up on the nuances of his promise.

While Corine planned her big celebration, Easy planned his revenge. There was no way he could honor his wife's wishes on this one. He needed to see Rock right away.

Somebody needed to pay for what had happened to his wife. And he was pretty sure he knew exactly who that someone was.

Chapter 14

Justice

Tuck picked up his phone in a huff. He was so annoyed that he almost ran off the road.

"Carlisle, where the hell have you been? Where are Elaina and the kids?" he belted out before he could even stop to listen. He had been trying to reach her all night.

"You lied, Agent Tucker," a strange male voice filtered through the phone.

"Who is this?" Tuck yelled. His voice surged up a few octaves. He was all over the road again. "Shit!" he cursed as he nearly sideswiped an SUV.

"Who is this?" he screamed as he threw on his hazards and pulled his car over. He looked at his phone screen one more time, just to make sure he had seen it right. CARLISLE, the screen flashed. He was right; it had been her phone that had called him.

"We had a deal, Agent Tucker, but you lied. Did you think we wouldn't be watching you? You said you would bring her to us, but then your lovesick, pussy-whipped ass just let her go."

Tuck shut his eyes tightly. Regret filled up inside him. He clenched his fists.

"Stokes! Where is Carlisle?" Tuck was out of the car, pacing now. Cars whizzed past him. He looked like a stranded motorist, walking the side of the highway in the rain.

There was laughter on the other end of the phone. "You have the nerve to ask me questions," the voice said snidely.

"Answer me! Where the fuck is Carlisle? My kids?" Tuck asked, his voice cracking as he nearly lost his grip on his cell phone. He was soaking wet from the pounding rain. He didn't even care.

"I guess you didn't really want to protect your family, Agent Tucker," the man continued.

It wasn't Stokes. Tuck would've recognized Stokes's voice by now. This man was younger; his voice was stronger.

"Where is my family?" Tuck screeched, feeling like someone had punched him in the solar plexus.

"Daddy! Help us!" Tuck heard his baby girl shout in the background of the call.

"No!" he screamed, falling to his knees. He looked up into the angry sky and pleaded for mercy from above. Only divine intervention could save his family right now.

The throngs of news reporters and policemen lining the outside of the Ponce Funeral Home gave the impression that a celebrity or politician had passed away. Each reporter and their camera crew jockeyed for the perfect spot in front of the doors for the money shot they all desired. They swarmed like angry bees, waiting to grill the former reputed drug kingpin, who was now burying two sons. The reports on the news had varied: Some said his sons had been killed as a result of an ongoing drug war with another borough; others said the crimes were revenge killings for DeSosa's past indiscretions. Police investigators were examining these incidents closely to see if the two murders were related. On the surface the MOs did not match at all.

Candy laughed at the circus that DeSosa was now forced to be a part of. She certainly enjoyed her role as the ringmaster.

The large crowd made the perfect cover and distraction. Candice made up her mind; she'd get in and out like the Grim Reaper. One fast sweep of blackness to finish the deed—the thought made her feel powerful, yet sad. What would she do when she no longer had revenge to fill her days?

Candice hadn't given that much thought to the future; she was still so consumed with the past and the present. She shook her head. No time to get fucking emotional right now.

Candice checked herself in the small driver's-side visor mirror one last time. An assassin in pink lip gloss; she had to giggle at that. The black wide brim hat, black oyster shell oval shades, black elbow-length gloves and nice fitted black sheath dress made her look very much the part of a high-class mourner. It was a look that suited her well.

Uncle Rock had always worn his black skullcap, black military-style jacket and black gloves as his signature kill-a-nigga wear. Candice thought this funeral get-up might be her signature look. Going to these funerals was starting to give her a rise. She knew it was sick, but it was satisfying, all the same.

Candice picked up the oversized black purse, checked for her weapon of choice and stepped out of the rental car. Her heels clicking on the pavement sounded off like gunshots. She liked that too. *Power. Power. Power.*

Candice looked down the street at the burgeoning crowd. They had no idea that in a few more minutes they'd all be in harm's way; she planned to come at them with a fury. A no-holds-barred display. Her last hit. She checked her little timer.

Hmph, only a few minutes left.

If she had timed everything correctly, DeSosa, Cyndi and the kids would be arriving soon. Candice couldn't miss that now, could she?

As soon as she reached the funeral home entrance, she felt her damn cell phone ringing inside. Only one person had her cell phone number, and that was Tuck. She really wasn't in the mood to speak with him right now. The phone stopped ringing and started back up, almost immediately. She didn't need to draw any extra attention to herself right now. She fished the phone out of her bag and hit the ignore button. Nothing could interrupt this moment.

Candice hadn't even made it to the edge of the crowd when the phone started to vibrate. Fuck! This time she felt a thunderbolt of anger spark in her chest. Candice stopped midstride and whirled around angrily. She was going to pick up that fucking phone and curse out Tuck.

"What do you want?" Candice said gruffly, but low enough as not to attract any undue attention.

"Candy! I need you!" Tuck cried out in pain.

Candice was struck dumb for a second; her body went stiff. Was he really crying?

"Tuck?" she whispered. Her eyebrows folded down onto the bridge of her nose.

"They have my family! They're going to kill my family!" he screamed at the top of his lungs.

His words snatched away Candice's breath. She made a hiccup noise and swallowed hard. A cold feeling shot through her body like somebody had pumped ice water into her veins. She gripped the phone tight and whirled around, her emotions on a collision course. She looked around wildly.

It was time.

Tuck was talking incoherently. He needed her to meet him right away. His family was in danger. His words were a confusing jumble in her ears.

Pandemonium broke out near the funeral home. Candice turned toward the commotion. Reporters started rushing in all directions; loud voices erupted from the crowd. Candice felt like someone had kicked her in the chest.

No! No! No!

Rolando DeSosa had arrived at his sons' funeral and Candice had missed her shot.

A bloodcurdling scream bounced off the walls of the long hotel hallway.

"Help! Help! Help!" the housekeeper screeched, running down the hall, her arms flailing.

Several nosy hotel patrons emerged from their rooms to investigate the noise. The brave ones ventured toward the source of the distress, but they quickly scrambled their asses back behind closed doors like cockroaches in the night. Within ten minutes the police were swarming the hotel.

The first uniformed officer to arrive on the scene had called in what he had observed: "Two DOAs, one white female, one black male, causes of death unknown. Both appear to have been dead for some time." Then he rushed into the bathroom and threw up. He knew he had probably contaminated something at the crime scene, but he couldn't help it. His stomach couldn't hold up to the smell of death that permeated the room.

When Candice prepared to turn onto the block of her hotel, she was stopped by a uniformed police officer. Confused, she rolled down her window like a dutiful citizen.

"Oh my goodness, Officer, what's going on?" She let her eyes dart to the police tape and all of the patrol cars and emergency service unit trucks that were parked haphazardly down the street.

"Ma'am, this street is blocked off. . . . Crime scene investigation is going on. You're going to have to come back later or use another route," the officer said perfunctorily.

"May I ask what happened?" She used her throatiest sex kitten voice. She could see the officer's face soften a bit. He looked like he knew better, but he was going to give the beautiful woman with the expensive sunglasses and voluptuous body the information, anyway.

"Two dead bodies in a hotel room is all I know," he answered, tapping the door of her car. Candice's surprise was genuine. She pushed her glasses back up to cover her wide-stretched eyes.

"I better get out of here then," she replied.

"Yes, ma'am, I'd say that's a good idea," the officer agreed.

She skidded away from the crime scene as quickly as possible. Her phone began to vibrate. Tuck was calling her again. "Shit!" she cursed under her breath. Her fucking nerves were really rattled now.

She reached over with one hand and snatched up the phone from the cup holder. He was supposed to meet her downtown, someplace crowded. BBQ's he had offered up as a meeting location. Candice had to change that now. She didn't have time to change her clothes or put on a new disguise. They'd have to come up with someplace that afforded a little more privacy.

"We need a different place to meet. Police are swarming all over my hotel. Your call," she announced. "Text me the address," she instructed before hanging up the call.

Candice busted a U-turn and headed in the opposite direction.

"Police are investigating the discovery of two dead bodies in a Brooklyn hotel room. A hotel housekeeper found the bodies when she went to clean the room earlier today. She reportedly told police, the person renting the room never asked for housekeeping services, and today was the first day the door was missing the Do Not Disturb sign," the anchorman stated. "When the housekeeper went inside, she found the body of a black male, mid to late thirties, and that of a white female in her early thirties. A police source that has asked not to be identified reported that the woman was wearing some sort of federal law enforcement badge around her neck. Police are not releasing information about the person who rented the room, but they say they have a lead in the case. In other news, the double funeral for the sons of reputed drug kingpin Rolando DeSosa was held in Brooklyn today. DeSosa, who arrived under a shroud of security, is the reported ruthless operator of a drug business that brings tens of millions of dollars' worth of crack cocaine to the streets of New York and L.A. Both of DeSosa's sons were murdered in separate incidents just in the last week. Police would not comment on whether they believe the family was being targeted."

Tuck sat in his old booth at the back of the small hole-in-the-wall, pub-style greasy spoon restaurant. He could hear the television reports, but he couldn't see the screen from where he sat. When he arrived at his old haunt, he had been sure to check his surroundings before he'd dipped inside. He had grown nostalgic as the smell of Greek food filled his nostrils.

"Ay," the owner of the restaurant sang when he recognized Tuck sitting in a quiet corner. The greeting made Tuck cringe; he didn't really want to be recognized. He leaned over the counter and told the owner he was waiting for someone and that he didn't want to be disturbed while he waited.

"Lika before, right?" the overweight, greasy-haired man asked in his thick Greek accent.

"Exactly," Tuck answered. He waited anxiously in the cramped booth for Candy to arrive.

Candy entered the small eatery and slid in across from him in a flurry. Candy looked beautiful, but he could see fear in her eyes.

Tuck looked tired. His eyes were still red-rimmed and puffy from crying. For some reason this did not make Tuck look weak in her eyes; a man who felt that passionate about saving his family was actually a trait worthy of admiration.

"Candy, you're the only person who can help me now. They've got my family, and they killed the DEA agent who tried to help me," Tuck confessed, his voice cracking again.

"Who are 'they,' Tuck?" Candice whispered.

Tuck hung his head. He knew if he confessed the truth, she might tell him to fuck off and then he'd be screwed.

"The CIA," he croaked out. He couldn't even look at her.

Candice curled her hands into fists. She leaned into the table. "Why the fuck does the CIA want to hurt your family, Tuck?" she whispered harshly. The wheels of her mind were already turning with ideas.

"Look, I made them believe I would help them find you so that they would leave my family alone. But I never had any intention of helping them. If I did, I would've led them to you yesterday when I gave you the file. I would've turned you over and walked away if I didn't care. I was trying to protect everyone involved, including you. You have to believe me, Candy." Tuck laid it all out there, not even taking a breath between his words. He didn't want to give her a chance to walk out on him.

Candice leaned back, feeling the busted-up leather of the booth digging into her shoulder. "You made a deal with the CIA, even after you knew what they did to my family?" Candice asked with all the condescension she could muster. How could he be *that* stupid?

"I told them to fuck off until they shot at my wife and kids," Tuck confessed. The words "wife and kids" rang in Candice's ear like a shrill alarm. She swallowed hard. Her sexual fantasies involving Tuck evaporated into thin air.

Fuckin' bastard.

"So you were going to hand me over to them until you realized you needed me more than they did? Fuck you, Tuck," Candice said as she moved to scoot out of the booth.

Tuck was out of his seat in a flash. He grabbed her arm. Candice whirled on him so fast—he didn't even have time to react. Her gun pressed into his chest bone.

"Fuckin' dare me," she taunted.

Tuck lifted his hands. He could see some of the patrons looking at them uneasily; though Candice was pretty careful not to brandish her weapon quite as openly.

"C'mon, Candy. You're not going to shoot me in the back of a fuckin' greasy spoon with eyewitnesses. Rock taught you better than that. Hear me out. I'm on your side. Right now, I bet those two dead bodies were found in your hotel room, which means, even if you used a fake name, the surveillance cameras will pick you up in that same outfit. There are cops fanned out all over the city looking for you right now," Tuck pleaded his case.

Candice inhaled and exhaled. She lowered her gun back under her hat, where she had hidden it on the seat next to her when she arrived.

"Sit down and let me tell you what I know. We have to work together. We can save my family, give you the man you really want to get, and then we all can get the fuck out of here." Tuck was trying to get her cooperation. He took her silence to mean consent.

"First things first—do you ever remember seeing anything in Barton's house containing the name Grayson Stokes? Anything?" Tuck asked seriously.

Candice had studied many things that she'd stolen from Uncle Rock's safe, but she couldn't be too sure.

"I—I . . . can't," she started.

Tuck leaned in; there was a look of panic on his face. "Please, Candy . . . you have to think. Please! My kids will be dead if we wait too long," he said solemnly. Tears were rimming his eyes. Candice looked across the table and bugged out as she saw the face of her father staring back at her. She had to shake off the hallucination. Tuck's passion about his kids reminded her so much of her father.

"I remember. I do remember that Uncle Rock had been studying Stokes as one of his marks," Candice confessed in a near whisper.

Tuck leaned back and clapped his hands together. Now they were getting somewhere.

"That man was one of the people who had tortured Uncle Rock when he was in the military back in the day. I read his stuff. . . . Uncle Rock wanted to kill Stokes, but something had him afraid," Candice told Tuck. "I have all of the information. It's a good fuckin' thing I never kept all my shit in that hotel room," Candice announced, digging her safe-deposit box key from her purse.

"Let's go, Candy! He has my family!" Tuck exclaimed, hopelessly optimistic. He wanted to hug and kiss her, but that could wait until after he found his wife and children. One thing Stokes had gotten right was that Candy was a force to be reckoned with. Candice and Tuck both shot up from the booth, ready for action. The greasy spoon owner had just started over to their table with Tuck's usual dish in hand. Tuck also noticed the man held Brubaker's favorite in his other hand.

"Not today. I can't stay." Tuck put his hand up, halting the man's ungainly stride. The man looked confused and crushed. "But here . . . remember what we talked about." Tuck dug into his pocket and placed a wad of cash in the man's dirty apron pocket. The money would more than cover the cost of the food and ensure the owner's silence when it came to other matters.

Cyndi DeSosa walked the long hallway that separated her and Arellio's wing of the home from her father-in-law's living quarters. Her heels clacked against the marble floors and she wrapped her arms around her body, fighting off the chills. Her face was still swollen from her ordeal; no amount of makeup could hide the fact that she was still grieving.

Cyndi hadn't even processed the heinous acts that had been carried out on her brother-in-law before she witnessed her own husband's death. It had all happened so fast. Cyndi didn't think she would ever get over the fact that her husband was standing in front of her one minute, and then dead the next. His brains had spewed out the front of his head and splattered onto her face, neck and clothing.

Cyndi had screamed until her throat was raw and bleeding. It had taken her two days of scrubbing her skin raw until she no longer saw or smelled his blood on her skin.

Cyndi was a shell of a person now. She felt cold down to her bones; and each time she closed her eyes, she replayed the scene in her mind like a movie. Cyndi took a daily cocktail of Valium, Zoloft and Ambien to try to stay sane, but she barely got an hour of sleep if she was lucky. She couldn't stand to be inside her house. Her husband had died in their living room; the room had been roped off like a quarantine area. No one was allowed in or out. Her house felt like a mausoleum.

Her bedroom reminded her that she was now a widow. Although she knew her husband was dead, she couldn't bear to pack away his belongings. Cyndi slept in the kids' room. She was always crying; and when she wasn't upset, it was only because she was so high from the drugs she took.

Little Rolando kept asking for his daddy. Each time he did, Cyndi would run to the bathroom to cry until she threw up. The baby was too young to understand; but each time Cyndi thought about her daughter growing up without a father, it made her double over in pain.

Cyndi arrived at DeSosa's quarters and folded her arms across her ample breasts. She cracked a half-hearted smile at DeSosa's guard, who stood in front of his bedroom door. The guard nodded in return, looking at her strangely.

"Is he okay?" she rasped, widening her red-rimmed eyes to look up at the hulk of a man. The man answered her in Spanish, stating he hadn't seen DeSosa all day.

"I'm going in to check on him. This is hard for all of us," Cyndi said softly; her throat was raw from all of the crying and screaming. The guard didn't dare resist her request for entrance. He stepped aside and opened the door for her.

Although DeSosa had said no visitors, he hadn't specified if his live-in daughter-in-law was considered a "visitor."

Cyndi stepped inside the darkened room and chills rushed over her body. There were three men inside. They were all sitting around a small table huddled together, whispering. The lights were dim and it was obvious Rolando had already gotten into bed.

Cyndi approached the men. *"Hola,"* she whispered.

They all looked at her in surprise.

"I want to have some time alone with him. Please give us a few minutes," she whispered.

The men looked at her and then at each other. No one was ready to say no to a grieving widow.

Cyndi immediately read their hesitation. "I just buried my fuckin' husband, and he just buried both of his sons. We are all we have left. . . . Surely, you fuckin' understand. Now get the fuck out," she commanded with all of the authority she could muster.

Stunned, the men scrambled up from their card game and hustled out of the room.

Cyndi watched and waited until she was alone with DeSosa. She walked to the back of the suite and pulled DeSosa's wheelchair away from his bedside. She tiptoed over to where he lay and watched him closely for a few minutes.

He was sleeping peacefully, probably because he'd been given a sedative cocktail to help him rest. Cyndi watched his slow breathing for a few minutes. She could definitely see her husband's face in her father-in-law's. Tears welled up in her eyes. She cupped her hand over her mouth to muffle her whimpers.

She couldn't understand how one man could cause so much death and destruction. Yes, she knew he sold drugs, but she had never wanted to admit until lately just how deep her father-in-law played in the drug game. When she'd called Dulce's cell phone to tell her that she was going to call the cops on her, Dulce had told her everything. Cyndi didn't believe it at first, but how would Dulce know such details about her family if she were concocting a story out of the blue?

Cyndi never had a chance to tell Arellio what she'd learned about his father. As far as Cyndi was concerned, Rolando DeSosa was scum of the earth. He was responsible for her husband's death too; there was no doubt in Cyndi's mind about that. She swallowed the golf ball–sized lump in the back of her throat and approached his sleeping form.

"*Papi* DeSosa," she whispered, shaking his arm softly with one of her trembling hands.

DeSosa lay stock-still.

"*Papi*," she said a bit louder, shaking him a bit more vigorously.

He let out a long sigh. At least she knew he was still breathing.

"*Papi* DeSosa," she called, moving her face lower, within his line of vision.

He finally stirred. His medication-dilated pupils rolled open; his eyelids slowly inched upward as if they were lead heavy. Cyndi felt a flash of relief.

"Are you awake now?" she asked, tapping his arm. He grunted. She could tell he was fighting against the drugs to wake up. She tapped him a few more times. He grunted again, but this time his eyes came all the way open.

"Cyndi?" DeSosa croaked out. His voice sounded like sandpaper against a wall. "Cyndi, is that you?" he asked, lifting his head slightly to look at her. He looked so weak, so feeble now. Cyndi had a hard time keeping the image of him as a cold-blooded murderer in her mind's eye.

"Yes, it's me," she said. Her voice cracked, and her eyes filled with tears. She watched him through blurry eyes, tilting her head to the side as if she were a child asking for a favor.

"What is it?" he asked. His eyes and brain were fully alert now. He reached out to touch her hand.

Cyndi snatched her hand back. She folded her arms across her chest. She didn't want his evil to rub off on her.

"What's the matter, Cyndi?" DeSosa asked more urgently this time.

"Why? Why? Why'd you do it?" she cried. Her shoulders shuddered as she was overcome with pain. "How could you? How. . . ," she wailed now, beyond words.

"What, Cyndi? What is it?" DeSosa asked, with raised eyebrows. He was growing worried about her. He looked down to the foot of his large bed. Then his eyes darted across the suite; he quickly noticed that his security detail was missing. He looked back at his daughter-in-law, and an uneasy feeling came over him. "Where is everybody, Cyndi?" he rasped.

"Was it worth it—losing your sons? How can you live with yourself?" Cyndi's voice was as hard and as sharp as steel.

DeSosa didn't have to ask her what she was talking about; she had discovered the sort of monster he'd become and was horrified to be living under the same roof. He didn't blame her. Tears ran out of the corners of his eyes. He was powerless. He couldn't even get himself out of bed. His head flopped back down on the pillow, defeated.

"You ruined a lot of lives! You killed women and children! You dragged your children into this! They only wanted to make you proud, so they joined you. They wanted to be like you! What kind of man are you?" Her voice was accusing. Her sobs changed to pure anger. "My kids don't have a father! I don't have a husband! All because of your selfish, evil ass!" she boomed through tears.

DeSosa didn't respond. He had made a lot of mistakes in his life and was paying for them now.

"Answer me!" Cyndi demanded. "Answer me, you fuckin' devil!" She could hear the security men at the door, trying to get inside. Cyndi's hand shook as she dug into her shirtfront. She pulled the small .22-caliber Smith & Wesson revolver from between her breasts and leveled it at her father-in-law. "You ruined too many lives. You ruined my life! You have to pay for your sins!" she belted out.

She could hear the footsteps rushing toward her. It was too late. With a rush of panic engulfing her, Cyndi fired off two shots.

DeSosa's eyes stared blankly at the ceiling. Her point-blank shots left two great gaping holes in his forehead.

DeSosa's security detail stormed the room and sounded off four shots. Cyndi's body dropped to the floor like a deflated balloon.

The men had arrived too late; their employer was dead and now so was his killer daughter-in-law.

Chapter 15

Day of Reckoning

Candice and Tuck both looked surprised when they arrived at their destination. The ranch-style 1960s-era house, located off a dirt road, and in the middle of a damn near forest, was not the place that one would expect the head honcho of the CIA to call home.

Candice peered out the car window. Tuck ducked his head and did the same.

"You sure you got this right?" Tuck asked doubtfully.

"Yeah," she mumbled, equally astonished.

"I guess that's why you should never judge a book by its position in the government, huh?" Tuck said lamely.

"Yeah, I was thinking it would be a mini-mansion for Stokes. Instead, we're looking at something one step above a fuckin' trailer home."

"Hey, it's your intel . . . not mine," Tuck clarified.

They went over their plan one more time. Tuck was shocked to learn that Candice knew so many techniques—slicing the pie, stacking up, fatal funnel and so on. In fact, she had ended up schooling him on a few techniques he'd never even learned in his numerous training classes.

"Remember, our main goal is to get him to say where my family is, and then he's all yours," Tuck told her.

Candice exhaled. Her gut was jumping and her heart was pounding. "You ready?" she asked Tuck.

"As ready as I'm ever gonna be," he responded.

She went for her door handle. He stopped her by placing his hand on her arm.

"Candy, no matter what happens in here, just know I was always on the side of good," Tuck said in all seriousness. His words sounded like parting words.

She cringed and mentally scolded herself for still having those feelings. "Same here. It was always just about justice for my family," she offered in return.

They exited the car at the same time.

"Down," Tuck whispered harshly. Her head was too high. He could see the black-clad men from Stokes's detail roving inside.

The simple ranch-style house had a very nondescript exterior. The grass was brown and looked like hay. What was left of the shrubbery barely resembled greenery at all. There were two small trees on either side of the front door, which surprised Tuck. As a spook he expected Stokes to know that those trees made for a great hiding spot for enemies lying in wait for an ambush.

Candice took her place behind the tree at the left of the door, and Tuck went to the one on the right. Candice popped her head up and peeked in the window. The blinds were drawn, but she could see through the small slits. There was only one man in black in the front foyer of the house. He was drinking a Coke, taking a break. Perfect.

Candice signaled to Tuck to move forward. He reached his long arm out and banged on the door. They both took cover behind their respective trees. Candice saw the man inside put the Coke down on the table. She lifted her hand up to tell Tuck that the man was coming.

Tuck stood upright, still out of sight. When the man pulled back the door, Tuck went into action. He put his gun to the man's head from the side. Candice did the same from the other side. "Shh," Tuck instructed the man. Candice dug in his shoulder holster and took his gun. She threw it in her bag. Then she took his handcuffs.

Tuck tackled the man down to the ground on his stomach, knocking the wind out of him. Before the man could even cough, Candice applied a few pressure points; in a matter of seconds, the man was knocked out. Tuck handcuffed the man's hands behind his back and flipped him over. Candice rushed to loosen his tie. Her hands were shaking fiercely with excitement.

"Hurry up before they miss him," Tuck whispered harshly. Finally the tie came free of the man's neck. Candice was able to double the material and made a gag.

Tuck dragged the man behind the bush he'd been hiding behind and propped him up against the house. Out of sight. Out of mind.

"C'mon," Candice said nervously. Tuck was taking too damn long; even she knew that. Tuck finally emerged. He waved his hands silently, signaling their next move.

Candice slipped inside the front door and went left, while Tuck went right. Backs up against the walls, they began the process of clearing the rooms until they found what they were looking for.

Candice's back hit up against a frame and it swayed precariously on the wall. *Shit!* She turned just a second to steady the picture. Tuck had made it to the doorway. He was waving and pointing, signaling to her that the other two bodyguards were nearby. He needed her to take one; he'd take the other.

Within seconds Candice was right up on his back; the hairs on his neck stood up in response to her rapid breaths behind his ear.

Now they both heard voices.

Candice's heart rate sped up.

The voices were getting closer.

"Where is this guy?" one of the men asked as his voice got louder and louder.

"Now!" Tuck whispered in her ear.

They both rushed through the opening to the hallway; Tuck's gun led the way. The unsuspecting bodyguard turned a sickening shade of white when he came face-to-face with the end of Tuck's gun. Tuck placed his fingers up to the man's lips, ordering his silence.

Tuck dragged the man down and Candice went to work. They handcuffed him, but they didn't bother with the tie this time.

Tuck put up his pointer finger to make the number one. He turned the same finger toward a doorway on the left. He was letting Candice know there was one more threat ahead. But there was still another door to the right, nearly diagonal from them. Candice knew this meant they'd have to split up. Somebody had to keep their eyeball on the other door to watch for any unaccounted-for and unknown threats. Tuck waved her on to the other door. Then he dipped into the door on the left.

Candice heard the man inside say, "What the . . ." but his words were clipped short. Obviously, the result of a quick blow to the back of his neck.

Candice was in front of the last door. She swallowed hard and tried to slow her rapid breathing. She reached down with her nonshooting hand and twisted the doorknob. The door clicked and it creaked open. With a two-handed grip, she slipped inside the room.

"I'm not ready to eat yet," the man inside scolded; his back was turned to the door. When he didn't get a response, he prepared his tongue to lambaste his shit-for-brains henchmen. He swiveled around in his chair with a scowl on his face. The man's eyes widened at the unexpected sight of the girl with the barrel of a gun aimed at his chest.

"Grayson Stokes? I'm Candice Hardaway. . . . I hear you been looking for me," she announced with the calm of Hannibal Lecter. He followed the gun with his eyes as it went up and came down with a *thwack* on his skull. Stokes growled before he slumped over like a sad heap of bones.

Candice was on the move. She dumped her bag out and retrieved the duct tape to make quick work with Stokes. With her gun tucked under her chin, she stepped behind his chair so he wouldn't have a visual of her. The tip of the tape was finally pulled up from the roll and she taped him to the chair.

"You don't have to do this," Stokes told her. She hit his ass in the shoulder with the end of her gun. His body involuntarily struggled against the restraints; his muscles pushed against his skin. Stokes had been caught off guard; he was attacked in his own home. He couldn't believe he was tied up and rendered helpless by a mere slip of a girl. With all of the things he had done in his life—the murders, the lies, the deceit—he would most likely not die of old age.

"You better start talking. Where are the kids?" Candice growled. Another blow sent a wavering shock over him. He could feel his teeth click in his mouth from the force of the blow. He wouldn't speak.

"Agggh!"

He let out a guttural scream as the end of her gun was driven into his testicles. He didn't know how much more of this he could take. Now he wished he couldn't feel anything . . . anywhere on his body. Another hit drew blood. A fit of coughing followed. The man whirled his head around, trying to will his lungs to fill back up with air. He was angry at his condition; his body had given out years ago, defying him over and over.

If Candice was anything like Barton, she had done her homework well and knew all about his weaknesses. The thought made him angry enough to kill. He gripped the handles of his own chair now. The large green veins in his hands bulged against his liver-spotted skin.

"Where the fuck are the kids?" Candice asked him, but he couldn't answer. He couldn't find the words.

His head—the pain trampling through it.

His ears—the shrill ringing.

It was all too much and rendered him speechless.

Blood leaked down the side of his face and into his left eye. The skin that was his eyebrow had parted wide, exposing pink flesh and white bone.

"Who are you?" he asked, sounding confused.

"Don't fuckin' act like you don't know who I am, you muthafucka!" Candice bellowed.

A maniacal laugh filled his ears.

"You don't know who I am? I thought you were like God. I thought you knew everything and controlled everyone." Her anger was as potent as the venom that dripped off each word.

"You're here to avenge your father? He deserved to die," Stokes said cruelly.

Candice walked over to her bag and retrieved something. Then she walked over to him and turned a box of salt upside down over his open wound. Tuck's Greek friend had hooked her up with a large bag of cooking salt, perfect for just this purpose.

"Agggh!"

Stokes was panting as the stinging from the salt sent a million tiny needles all over his body. Another hit from the gun rocked through his cranium. This time Stokes barely held on to his consciousness.

"I will ask you again for the truth. Where the fuck is Tucker's family?" Candice continued to pour more salt over his open wounds.

The man opened his lips and began to speak, but his tone was a weak whisper.

"I knew you would come. I had been expecting you," Stokes barely managed.

Candice's hands shook now; anticipation was making her antsy. She wanted to blow his fucking brains out, but she had to find out where Tuck's kids were first.

"I knew all of this time you would come," Stokes whispered again. Then his head dropped forward, and his chin hit his chest.

"Good. Then you should've been expecting this," Candice said in an even tone as she lifted her weapon. The man looked up at her out of battered eyes. He locked gazes with Candice. Stokes tried to hold back a coughing fit, but he lost that battle.

"How did you find me?" he asked weakly.

"Don't worry about that!" Candice responded. She was enraged. "Where the fuck are the kids?" She hit him again across the face.

Stokes's mouth filled with blood, making him look like a *Twilight* film extra.

Candice could swear the man was smiling. This angered her even further.

"Wh—why . . . don't you . . . as-ask Agent Tucker where his family is?" Stokes wheezed.

Candice swung her body around. Tuck was standing in the doorway; sweat was dripping down his face.

"He's not telling me anything. Our salt trick didn't work." Candice turned to Tuck.

Stokes began laughing; then another fit of that same cough that Candice recognized from Uncle Rock. Tuck moved into the room but didn't speak. Three goons in black were behind him.

Candice lifted her gun and leveled it at all of them.

Stokes started laughing again. "Can't you see what's going on here, Candy girl?" Stokes asked weakly, true merriment in his voice.

"Shut the fuck up and tell me where the kids are," Candice barked. Her voice was cracking. Things were going downhill fast.

"Ask Tucker," Stokes demanded. His voice was getting stronger now.

Tuck just stood there, silent as a church mouse.

No, not again.

"What is he talking about, Tuck?" Her gun was aimed straight for his head now.

Tuck let out a long breath.

"Don't you know that Agent Tucker would do anything to save his job? From day one he sold his soul to the very devil to make a name for himself. He used you, his wife and even his kids as pawns," Stokes rasped out. He was coughing and wheezing for breath between nearly every word.

Candice's body became engulfed in heat as the gravity of the situation sank in.

"We used you, Candy. All of the people who knew about Operation Easy In are now gone. We couldn't afford for that kind of information to get out," Stokes continued.

Candice looked at Tuck; hurt was evident in her eyes. She readjusted the grip on her gun.

"You better start fuckin' talking, Tuck. You better tell me that muthafucka is lying just to save his own ass!" she screamed. Candice was still holding out hope that this conspiracy theory was just a fluke—that Tuck hadn't sold her out to Stokes to save his own ass.

Tuck didn't say a word. Candice swallowed hard. His silence was louder than any verbal confirmation of the truth.

"You fuckin' traitor bitch!" she screeched. Hot tears were running down her cheeks. "I can't believe I let myself fall for your lies! I should've known a bastard that would go undercover for a year and not care to check on his family was a piece of shit!" Candice screamed. Her gun hand was shaking now, wavering dangerously between Stokes and Tucker. She didn't know which one she wanted to take out first.

"Agent Tucker agreed to lure you here. He knew he could get you here with a story about saving his family. He really did have to save his family from us. You're a Hardaway through and through," Stokes said cruelly. "I guess he sacrificed more than some fling with a revenge-filled little girl," Stokes cackled.

"Shut the fuck up!" Candice screamed, and with one motion she turned and shot Stokes in the head. Blood splattered everywhere. Her gun was back on Tuck within two seconds.

"That's what I came here for. Nothing else matters now," Candice cried, leveling her gun at Tuck's head. He lifted his gun and leveled it at her head in return.

"You know your father was down with the motherfucker who killed my father in the line of fucking duty," Tuck gritted out. "I found that out by reading over your father's fucking books. You're not the only one who craves justice." Tuck's weak eye closed instinctively. *Shoot until the threat is eliminated. Eliminated. Eliminated.* Tuck chanted this mantra in his head.

Candice moved the pad of her finger. *Trigger. Trigger. Trigger.* She was chanting her coda inside her head.

Bang! Bang!

Candice and Tucker lay in a pool of shared blood, like a modern-day version of *Romeo and Juliet,* waiting for their last breaths to leave their bodies. Revenge had not been nearly as sweet and satisfying as they had imagined it to be.

The darkness that engulfed them was cold and unwelcoming. The aftertaste of regret in one's mouth was always bitter.